"The most heartwarm... space opera I've enjoyed in a long time. Martha Wells is the best writer of lovable snarky gender-subversive killing machines out there!"   —N. K. Jemisin

"We are all a little bit Murderbot."   —NPR

"If you need something light, a little violent, and laugh-out-loud hilarious, dive into this series: You may find that you have more in common with Murderbot than you think."
—Liz Braswell, *The Wall Street Journal*

"Readers won't miss the wall-to-wall action that defined the series from its beginning. The characters and the world-building remain engrossing and rewarding."
—*Booklist* (starred review)

"I might have a little bit of a thing for a robot. Its name is Murderbot.... *Network Effect* [is] great."   —*Wired*

"I can think of no better company than this paranoid android."   —*New Scientist*

"Murderbot, with its on-point observations and addictive interior monologues, is easily one of my favorite characters in SF.... Highly recommended."
—Charles de Lint, *The Magazine of
Fantasy & Science Fiction*

"I could read about Murderbot all *week*."   —*Locus*

ALSO BY MARTHA WELLS

THE MURDERBOT DIARIES

VOL. 1

All Systems Red

Artificial Condition

MARTHA WELLS

TOR PUBLISHING GROUP

NEW YORK

THE MURDERBOT DIARIES VOL. 1

All Systems Red copyright © 2017 by Martha Wells
Artificial Condition copyright © 2018 by Martha Wells

Excerpt from *Rogue Protocol* copyright © 2018 by Martha Wells

A Tordotcom Book
Published by Tom Doherty Associates / Tor Publishing Group
120 Broadway
New York, NY 10271

www.torpublishinggroup.com

Tor® is a registered trademark of
Macmillan Publishing Group, LLC.

ISBN 978-1-250-38982-4 (trade paperback)

Our books may be purchased in bulk for promotional, educational, or business use. Please contact your local bookseller or the Macmillan Corporate and Premium Sales Department at 1-800-221-7945, extension 5442, or by email at MacmillanSpecialMarkets@macmillan.com.

First Edition: 2025

Printed in the United States of America

0 9 8 7 6 5 4 3 2 1

All Systems Red

Chapter One

I COULD HAVE BECOME a mass murderer after I hacked my governor module, but then I realized I could access the combined feed of entertainment channels carried on the company satellites. It had been well over 35,000 hours or so since then, with still not much murdering, but probably, I don't know, a little under 35,000 hours of movies, serials, books, plays, and music consumed. As a heartless killing machine, I was a terrible failure.

I was also still doing my job, on a new contract, and hoping Dr. Volescu and Dr. Bharadwaj finished their survey soon so we could get back to the habitat and I could watch episode 397 of *Rise and Fall of Sanctuary Moon.*

I admit I was distracted. It was a boring contract so far and I was thinking about backburnering the status alert channel and trying to access music on the entertainment feed without HubSystem logging the extra activity. It was trickier to do it in the field than it was in the habitat.

This assessment zone was a barren stretch of coastal island, with low, flat hills rising and falling and thick greenish-black grass up to my ankles, not much in the way of flora or fauna, except a bunch of different-sized birdlike things and some puffy floaty things that were harmless as far as we knew. The coast was dotted with big bare craters, one of which Bharadwaj and Volescu were taking samples in. The planet had a ring, which from our current position dominated the horizon when you looked out to sea. I was looking at the sky and mentally poking at the feed when the bottom of the crater exploded.

I didn't bother to make a verbal emergency call. I sent the visual feed from my field camera to Dr. Mensah's, and jumped down into the crater. As I scrambled down the sandy slope, I could already hear Mensah over the emergency comm channel, yelling at someone to get the hopper in the air now. They were about ten kilos away, working on another part of the island, so there was no way they were going to get here in time to help.

Conflicting commands filled my feed but I didn't pay attention. Even if I hadn't borked my own governor module, the emergency feed took priority, and it was chaotic, too, with the automated HubSystem wanting data and trying to send me data I didn't need yet and Mensah sending me telemetry from the hopper. Which I also didn't need, but it was easier to ignore than HubSystem simultaneously demanding answers and trying to supply them.

In the middle of all that, I hit the bottom of the crater. I have small energy weapons built into both arms, but the one I went for was the big projectile weapon clamped to my back. The hostile that had just exploded up out of the ground had a really big mouth, so I felt I needed a really big gun.

I dragged Bharadwaj out of its mouth and shoved myself in there instead, and discharged my weapon down its throat and then up toward where I hoped the brain would be. I'm not sure if that all happened in that order; I'd have to replay my own field camera feed. All I knew was that I had Bharadwaj, and it didn't, and it had disappeared back down the tunnel.

She was unconscious and bleeding through her suit from massive wounds in her right leg and side. I clamped the weapon back into its harness so I could lift her with both arms. I had lost the armor on my left arm and a lot of the flesh underneath, but my nonorganic parts were still working. Another burst of commands from the governor module came through and I backburnered it without bothering to decode them. Bharadwaj, not having nonorganic parts and not as easily repaired as me, was definitely a priority here and I was mainly interested in what the MedSystem was trying to tell me on the emergency feed. But first I needed to get her out of the crater.

During all this, Volescu was huddled on the churned

up rock, losing his shit, not that I was unsympathetic. I was far less vulnerable in this situation than he was and I wasn't exactly having a great time either. I said, "Dr. Volescu, you need to come with me now."

He didn't respond. MedSystem was advising a tranq shot and *blah blah blah,* but I was clamping one arm on Dr. Bharadwaj's suit to keep her from bleeding out and supporting her head with the other, and despite everything I only have two hands. I told my helmet to retract so he could see my human face. If the hostile came back and bit me again, this would be a bad mistake, because I did need the organic parts of my head. I made my voice firm and warm and gentle, and said, "Dr. Volescu, it's gonna be fine, okay? But you need to get up and come help me get her out of here."

That did it. He shoved to his feet and staggered over to me, still shaking. I turned my good side toward him and said, "Grab my arm, okay? Hold on."

He managed to loop his arm around the crook of my elbow and I started up the crater towing him, holding Bharadwaj against my chest. Her breathing was rough and desperate and I couldn't get any info from her suit. Mine was torn across my chest so I upped the warmth on my body, hoping it would help. The feed was quiet now, Mensah having managed to use her leadership priority to mute everything but MedSystem and the hopper, and all

I could hear on the hopper feed was the others frantically shushing each other.

The footing on the side of the crater was lousy, soft sand and loose pebbles, but my legs weren't damaged and I got up to the top with both humans still alive. Volescu tried to collapse and I coaxed him away from the edge a few meters, just in case whatever was down there had a longer reach than it looked.

I didn't want to put Bharadwaj down because something in my abdomen was severely damaged and I wasn't sure I could pick her up again. I ran my field camera back a little and saw I had gotten stabbed with a tooth, or maybe a cilia. Did I mean a cilia or was that something else? They don't give murderbots decent education modules on anything except murdering, and even those are the cheap versions. I was looking it up in HubSystem's language center when the little hopper landed nearby. I let my helmet seal and go opaque as it settled on the grass.

We had two standard hoppers: a big one for emergencies and this little one for getting to the assessment locations. It had three compartments: one big one in the middle for the human crew and two smaller ones to each side for cargo, supplies, and me. Mensah was at the controls. I started walking, slower than I normally would have because I didn't want to lose Volescu. As the ramp started to drop, Pin-Lee and Arada jumped out and I switched to voice comm to say, "Dr. Mensah, I can't let go of her suit."

It took her a second to realize what I meant. She said hurriedly, "That's all right, bring her up into the crew cabin."

Murderbots aren't allowed to ride with the humans and I had to have verbal permission to enter. With my cracked governor there was nothing to stop me, but not letting anybody, especially the people who held my contract, know that I was a free agent was kind of important. Like, not having my organic components destroyed and the rest of me cut up for parts important.

I carried Bharadwaj up the ramp into the cabin, where Overse and Ratthi were frantically unclipping seats to make room. They had their helmets off and their suit hoods pulled back, so I got to see their horrified expressions when they took in what was left of my upper body through my torn suit. I was glad I had sealed my helmet.

This is why I actually like riding with the cargo. Humans and augmented humans in close quarters with murderbots is too awkward. At least, it's awkward for this murderbot. I sat down on the deck with Bharadwaj in my lap while Pin-Lee and Arada dragged Volescu inside.

We left two pacs of field equipment and a couple of instruments behind, still sitting on the grass where Bharadwaj and Volescu had been working before they went down to the crater for samples. Normally I'd help carry them, but MedSystem, which was monitoring Bharadwaj through what was left of her suit, was pretty clear that letting go of her would be a bad idea. But no one mentioned the equipment. Leaving easily replaceable items behind may seem obvious in an emergency, but I had been on contracts where the clients would have told me to put the bleeding human down to go get the stuff.

On this contract, Dr. Ratthi jumped up and said, "I'll get the cases!"

I yelled, "No!" which I'm not supposed to do; I'm always supposed to speak respectfully to the clients, even when they're about to accidentally commit suicide. Hub-System could log it and it could trigger punishment through the governor module. If it wasn't hacked.

Fortunately, the rest of the humans yelled "No!" at the same time, and Pin-Lee added, "For fuck's sake, Ratthi!"

Ratthi said, "Oh, no time, of course. I'm sorry!" and hit the quick-close sequence on the hatch.

So we didn't lose our ramp when the hostile came up under it, big mouth full of teeth or cilia or whatever chewing right through the ground. There was a great view of it on the hopper's cameras, which its system helpfully sent straight to everybody's feed. The humans screamed.

Mensah pushed us up into the air so fast and hard I nearly leaned over, and everybody who wasn't on the floor ended up there.

In the quiet afterward, as they gasped with relief, Pin-Lee said, "Ratthi, if you get yourself killed—"

"You'll be very cross with me, I know." Ratthi slid down the wall a little more and waved weakly at her.

"That's an order, Ratthi, don't get yourself killed," Mensah said from the pilot's seat. She sounded calm, but I have security priority, and I could see her racing heartbeat through MedSystem.

Arada pulled out the emergency medical kit so they could stop the bleeding and try to stabilize Bharadwaj. I tried to be as much like an appliance as possible, clamping the wounds where they told me to, using my failing body temperature to try to keep her warm, and keeping my head down so I couldn't see them staring at me.

———

```
performance reliability at 60% and dropping
```

Our habitat is a pretty standard model, seven interconnected domes set down on a relatively flat plain above a narrow river valley, with our power and recycling system connected on one side. We had an environmental system, but no air locks, as the planet's atmosphere was breathable, just not particularly good for humans for the long term. I don't know why, because it's one of those things I'm not contractually obligated to care about.

We picked the location because it's right in the middle of the assessment area, and while there are trees scattered through the plain, each one is fifteen or so meters tall, very skinny, with a single layer of spreading canopy, so it's hard for anything approaching to use them as cover. Of course, that didn't take into account anything approaching via tunnel.

We have security doors on the habitat for safety but HubSystem told me the main one was already open as the hopper landed. Dr. Gurathin had a lift gurney ready and guided it out to us. Overse and Arada had managed to get Bharadwaj stabilized, so I was able to put her down on it and follow the others into the habitat.

The humans headed for Medical and I stopped to send the little hopper commands to lock and seal itself, then I locked the outer doors. Through the security feed, I told the drones to widen our perimeter so I'd have more warning if something big came at us. I also set some monitors on the seismic sensors to alert me to anomalies just in case the hypothetical something big decided to tunnel in.

After I secured the habitat, I went back to what was

called the security ready room, which was where weapons, ammo, perimeter alarms, drones, and all the other supplies pertaining to security were stored, including me. I shed what was left of the armor and on MedSystem's advice sprayed wound sealant all over my bad side. I wasn't dripping with blood, because my arteries and veins seal automatically, but it wasn't nice to look at. And it hurt, though the wound seal did numb it a little. I had already set an eight-hour security interdiction through HubSystem, so nobody could go outside without me, and then set myself as off-duty. I checked the main feed but no one was filing any objections to that.

I was freezing because my temperature controls had given out at some point on the way here, and the protective skin that went under my armor was in pieces. I had a couple of spares but pulling one on right now would not be practical, or easy. The only other clothing I had was a uniform I hadn't worn yet, and I didn't think I could get it on, either. (I hadn't needed the uniform because I hadn't been patrolling inside the habitat. Nobody had asked for that, because with only eight of them and all friends, it would be a stupid waste of resources, namely me.) I dug around one-handed in the storage case until I found the extra human-rated medical kit I'm allowed in case of emergencies, and opened it and got the survival blanket out. I wrapped up in it, then climbed into the plastic bed of my cubicle. I let the door seal as the white light flickered on.

It wasn't much warmer in there, but at least it was cozy. I connected myself to the resupply and repair leads, leaned back against the wall and shivered. MedSystem helpfully informed me that my performance reliability was now at 58 percent and dropping, which was not a surprise. I could definitely repair in eight hours, and probably mostly regrow my damaged organic components, but at 58 percent, I doubted I could get any analysis done in the meantime. So I set all the security feeds to alert me if anything tried to eat the habitat and started to call up the supply of media I'd downloaded from the entertainment feed. I hurt too much to pay attention to anything with a story, but the friendly noise would keep me company.

Then someone knocked on the cubicle door.

I stared at it and lost track of all my neatly arrayed inputs. Like an idiot, I said, "Uh, yes?"

Dr. Mensah opened the door and peered in at me. I'm not good at guessing actual humans' ages, even with all the visual entertainment I watch. People in the shows don't usually look much like people in real life, at least not in the good shows. She had dark brown skin and lighter brown hair, cut very short, and I'm guessing she wasn't young or she wouldn't be in charge. She said, "Are you all right? I saw your status report."

"Uh." That was the point where I realized that I should have just not answered and pretended to be in stasis. I pulled the blanket around my chest, hoping she hadn't seen any of the missing chunks. Without the armor holding me together, it was much worse. "Fine."

So, I'm awkward with actual humans. It's not paranoia about my hacked governor module, and it's not them; it's me. I know I'm a horrifying murderbot, and they know it, and it makes both of us nervous, which makes me even more nervous. Also, if I'm not in the armor then it's because I'm wounded and one of my organic parts may fall off and plop on the floor at any moment and no one wants to see that.

"Fine?" She frowned. "The report said you lost 20 percent of your body mass."

"It'll grow back," I said. I know to an actual human I probably looked like I was dying. My injuries were the equivalent of a human losing a limb or two plus most of their blood volume.

"I know, but still." She eyed me for a long moment, so long I tapped the security feed for the mess, where the non-wounded members of the group were sitting around the table talking. They were discussing the possibility of more underground fauna and wishing they had intoxicants. That seemed pretty normal. She continued, "You were very good with Dr. Volescu. I don't think the others realized . . . They were very impressed."

"It's part of the emergency med instructions, calming victims." I tugged the blanket tighter so she didn't see anything awful. I could feel something lower down leaking.

"Yes, but the MedSystem was prioritizing Bharadwaj and didn't check Volescu's vital signs. It didn't take into account the shock of the event, and it expected him to be able to leave the scene on his own."

On the feed it was clear that the others had reviewed Volescu's field camera video. They were saying things like *I didn't even know it had a face.* I'd been in armor since we arrived, and I hadn't unsealed the helmet when I was around them. There was no specific reason. The only part of me they would have seen was my head, and it's standard, generic human. But they didn't want to talk to me and I definitely didn't want to talk to them; on duty it would distract me and off duty . . . I didn't want to talk to them. Mensah had seen me when she signed the rental contract. But she had barely looked at me and I had barely looked at her because again, murderbot + actual human = awkwardness. Keeping the armor on all the time cuts down on unnecessary interaction.

I said, "It's part of my job, not to listen to the System feeds when they . . . make mistakes." That's why you need constructs, SecUnits with organic components. But she should know that. Before she accepted delivery of me, she had logged about ten protests, trying to get out of having to have me. I didn't hold it against her. I wouldn't have wanted me either.

Seriously, I don't know why I didn't just say *you're welcome* and *please get out of my cubicle so I can sit here and leak in peace.*

"All right," she said, and looked at me for what objectively I knew was 2.4 seconds and subjectively about twenty excruciating minutes. "I'll see you in eight hours. If you need anything before then, please send me an alert on the feed." She stepped back and let the door slide closed.

It left me wondering what they were all marveling at so I called up the recording of the incident. Okay, wow. I had talked to Volescu all the way up the side of the crater. I had been mostly concerned with the hopper's trajectory and Bharadwaj not bleeding out and what might come out of that crater for a second try; I hadn't been listening to myself, basically. I had asked him if he had kids. It was boggling. Maybe I had been watching too much media. (He did have kids. He was in a four-way marriage and had seven, all back home with his partners.)

All my levels were too elevated now for a rest period, so I decided I might as well get some use out of it and look at the other recordings. Then I found something weird. There was an "abort" order in the HubSystem command feed, the one that controlled, or currently believed it controlled, my governor module. It had to be a glitch. It didn't matter, because when MedSystem has priority—

```
          performance reliability at 39%
    stasis initiated for emergency repair sequence
```

Chapter Two

WHEN I WOKE UP, I was mostly all there again, and up to 80 percent efficiency and climbing. I checked all the feeds immediately, in case the humans wanted to go out, but Mensah had extended the security interdict on the habitat for another four hours. Which was a relief, since it would give me time to get back up to the 98 percent range. But there was also a notice for me to report to her. That had never happened before. But maybe she wanted to go over the hazard info package and figure out why it hadn't warned us about the underground hostile. I was wondering a little about that myself.

Their group was called PreservationAux and it had bought an option on this planet's resources, and the survey trip was to see if it was worth bidding on a full share. Knowing about things on the planet that might eat them while they're trying to do whatever it is they're doing was kind of important.

I don't care much about who my clients are or what they're trying to accomplish. I knew this group was from a freehold planet but I hadn't bothered to look up the specifics. Freehold meant it had been terraformed and colonized but wasn't affiliated with any corporate confederations. Basically *freehold* generally meant *shitshow* so I hadn't been expecting much from them. But they were surprisingly easy to work for.

I cleaned all the stray fluids off my new skin, then climbed out of the cubicle. That was when I realized I hadn't put the pieces of my armor up and it was all over the floor, covered with my fluids and Bharadwaj's blood. No wonder Mensah had looked into the cubicle; she had probably thought I was dead in there. I put it all back into its slots in the reclaimer for repair.

I had an alternate set, but it was still packed into storage and it would take extra time to pull it out and do the diagnostics and the fitting. I hesitated over the uniform, but the security feed would have notified Mensah that I was awake, so I needed to get out there.

It was based on a standard research group's uniforms, and meant to be comfortable inside the habitat: knit gray pants, long-sleeved T-shirt, and a jacket, like the exercise clothes humans and augmented humans wore, plus soft shoes. I put it on, tugged the sleeves down over the gunports on my forearms, and went out into the habitat.

I went through two interior secure doors to the crew area, and found them in the main hub in a huddle around a console, looking at one of the hovering displays. They were all there except Bharadwaj, who was still in the infirmary, and Volescu, who was sitting in there with her. There were mugs and empty meal packets on some of the consoles. I'm not cleaning that up unless I'm given a direct order.

Mensah was busy so I stood and waited.

Ratthi glanced at me, and then did a startled double take. I had no idea how to react. This is why I prefer wearing the armor, even inside the habitat where it's unnecessary and can just get in the way. Human clients usually like to pretend I'm a robot and that's much easier in the armor. I let my eyes unfocus and pretended I was running a diagnostic on something.

Clearly bewildered, Ratthi said, "Who is this?"

They all turned to look at me. All but Mensah, who was sitting at the console with the interface pressed to her forehead. It was clear that even after seeing my face on Volescu's camera video, they didn't recognize me without the helmet. So then I had to look at them and say, "I'm your SecUnit."

They all looked startled and uncomfortable. Almost as uncomfortable as I did. I wished I'd waited to pull the spare armor out.

Part of it is, they didn't want me here. Not here in their hub, but here on the planet. One of the reasons the bond company requires it, besides slapping more expensive markups on their clients, is that I was recording all their conversations all the time, though I wasn't monitoring anything I didn't need to do a half-assed version of my job. But the company would access all those recordings and data mine them for anything they could sell. No, they don't tell people that. Yes, everyone does know it. No, there's nothing you can do about it.

After a subjective half hour and an objective 3.4 seconds, Dr. Mensah turned, saw me, and lowered the interface. She said, "We were checking the hazard report for this region to try to learn why that thing wasn't listed under hazardous fauna. Pin-Lee thinks the data has been altered. Can you examine the report for us?"

"Yes, Dr. Mensah." I could have done this in my cubicle and we could have all saved the embarrassment. Anyway, I picked up the feed she was watching from HubSystem and started to check the report.

It was basically a long list of pertinent info and warnings on the planet and specifically the area where our habitat was, with emphasis on weather, terrain, flora, fauna, air quality, mineral deposits, possible hazards related to any and all of those, with connections to subreports with more detailed information. Dr. Gurathin, the least talkative one, was an augmented human and had his own implanted interface. I could feel him poking around in the data, while the others, using the touch interfaces, were just distant ghosts. I had a lot more processing power than he did, though.

I thought they were being paranoid; even with the interfaces you actually have to read the words, preferably all the words. Sometimes non-augmented humans don't do that. Sometimes augmented humans don't do it either.

But as I checked the general warning section, I noticed something was odd about the formatting. A quick comparison with the other parts of the report told me that yeah, something had been removed, a connection to a subreport broken. "You're right," I said, distracted as I rifled through data storage looking for the missing piece. I couldn't find it; it wasn't just a broken connection, somebody had actually deleted the subreport. That was supposed to be impossible with this type of planetary survey package, but I guess it wasn't as impossible as all that. "Something's been deleted from the warnings and the section on fauna."

The reaction to that in general was pretty pissed off. There were some loud complaints from Pin-Lee and Overse and dramatic throwing-hands-in-the-air from Ratthi. But, like I said, they were all friends and a lot less restrained with each other than my last set of contractual obligations. It was why, if I forced myself to admit it, I had actually been enjoying this contract, up until something tried to eat me and Bharadwaj.

SecSystem records everything, even inside the sleeping cabins, and I see everything. That's why it's easier to pretend I'm a robot. Overse and Arada were a couple, but from the way they acted they'd always been one, and they were best friends with Ratthi. Ratthi had an unrequited thing for Pin-Lee, but didn't act stupid about it. Pin-Lee was exasperated a lot, and tossed things around when the others weren't there, but it wasn't about Ratthi. I thought that being under the company's eye affected her more than the others. Volescu admired Mensah to the point where he might have a crush on her. Pin-Lee did, too, but she and Bharadwaj flirted occasionally in an old comfortable way that suggested it had been going on for a long time. Gurathin was the only loner, but he seemed to like being with the others. He had a small, quiet smile, and they all seemed to like him.

It was a low-stress group, they didn't argue much or antagonize each other for fun, and were fairly restful to be around, as long as they didn't try to talk or interact with me in any way.

Mid expression of frustration, Ratthi said, "So we have no way to know if that creature was an aberration or if they live at the bottom of all those craters?"

Arada, who was one of the biology specialists, said, "You know, I bet they do. If those big avians we saw on the scans land on those barrier islands frequently, that creature might be preying on them."

"It would explain what the craters are doing there," Mensah said more thoughtfully. "That would be one anomaly out of the way, at least."

"But who removed that subreport?" Pin-Lee said, which I agreed was the more important question here. She turned to me with one of those abrupt movements that I had taught myself not to react to. "Can the HubSystem be hacked?"

From the outside, I had no idea. It was as easy as breathing to do it from the inside, with the built-in interfaces in my own body. I had hacked it as soon as it had come online when we set up the habitat. I had to; if it monitored the governor module and my feed like it was supposed to, it could lead to a lot of awkward questions and me being stripped for parts. "As far as I know, it's possible," I said. "But it's more likely the report was damaged before you received the survey package."

Lowest bidder. Trust me on that one.

There were groans and general complaining about having to pay high prices for shitty equipment. (I don't take it personally.) Mensah said, "Gurathin, maybe you and Pin-Lee can figure out what happened." Most of my clients only know their specialties, and there's no reason to send a system specialist along on a survey trip. The company supplies all the systems and attachments (the medical equipment, the drones, me, etc.) and will maintain it as part of the over-all package the clients purchase. But Pin-Lee seemed to be a gifted amateur at system interpretation, and Gurathin had an advantage with his internal interface. Mensah added, "In the meantime, does the DeltFall Group have the same survey package as we do?"

I checked. HubSystem thought it was likely, but we knew what its opinion was worth now. "Probably," I said. DeltFall was another survey group, like us, but they were on a continent on the opposite side of the planet. They were a bigger operation and had been dropped off by a different ship, so the humans hadn't met in person, but they talked over the comm occasionally. They weren't part of my contract and had their own SecUnits, the standard one per ten clients. We were supposed to be able to call on each other in emergencies, but being half a planet apart put a natural damper on that.

Mensah leaned back in her chair and steepled her fingers. "All right, this is what we'll do. I want you each to check the individual sections of the survey package for your specialties. Try to pinpoint any more missing information. When we have a partial list, I'll call DeltFall and see if they can send us the files."

That sounded like a great plan, in that it didn't involve me. I said, "Dr. Mensah, do you need me for anything else?"

She turned her chair to face me. "No, I'll call if we have any questions." I had worked for some contracts that would have kept me standing here the entire day and night cycle, just on the off chance they wanted me to do something and didn't want to bother using the feed to call me. Then she added, "You know, you can stay here in the crew area if you want. Would you like that?"

They all looked at me, most of them smiling. One disadvantage in wearing the armor is that I get used to opaquing the faceplate. I'm out of practice at controlling my expression. Right now I'm pretty sure it was somewhere in the region of stunned horror, or maybe appalled horror.

Mensah sat up, startled. She said hurriedly, "Or not, you know, whatever you like."

I said, "I need to check the perimeter," and managed to turn and leave the crew area in a totally normal way and not like I was fleeing from a bunch of giant hostiles.

———————

Back in the safety of the ready room, I leaned my head against the plastic-coated wall. Now they knew their murderbot didn't want to be around them any more than they wanted to be around it. I'd given a tiny piece of myself away.

That can't happen. I have too much to hide, and letting one piece go means the rest isn't as protected.

I shoved away from the wall and decided to actually do some work. The missing subreport made me a little cautious. Not that there were any directives about it. My education modules were such cheap crap; most of the useful things I knew about security I learned from the edutainment programming on the entertainment feeds. (That's another reason why they have to require these research groups and mining and biology and tech companies to rent one of us or they won't guarantee the bond; we're cheaply produced and we suck. Nobody would hire one of us for non-murdering purposes unless they had to.)

Once I got my extra suit skin and spare set of armor on, I walked the perimeter and compared the current readings of the terrain and the seismic scans to the one we took when we first arrived. There were some notes in the feed from Ratthi and Arada, that fauna like the one we were now calling Hostile One might have made all the anomalous craters in the survey area. But nothing had changed around the habitat.

I also checked to make sure both the big hopper and the little hopper had their full complement of emergency supplies. I packed them in there myself days ago, but I was mainly checking to make sure the humans hadn't done anything stupid with them since the last time I checked.

I did everything I could think of to do, then finally let myself go on standby while I caught up on my serials. I'd watched three episodes of *Sanctuary Moon* and was fast forwarding through a sex scene when Dr. Mensah sent me some images through the feed. (I don't have any gender or sex-related parts (if a construct has those you're a sexbot in a brothel, not a murderbot) so maybe that's why I find sex scenes boring. Though I think that even if I did have sex-related parts I would find them boring.) I took a look at the images in Mensah's message, then saved my place in the serial.

Confession time: I don't actually know where we are. We have, or are supposed to have, a complete satellite map of the planet in the survey package. That was how the humans decided where to do their assessments. I hadn't looked at the maps yet and I'd barely looked at the survey package. In my defense, we'd been here twenty-two planetary days and I hadn't had to do anything but stand around watching humans make scans or take samples of dirt, rocks, water, and leaves. The sense of urgency just wasn't there. Also, you may have noticed, I don't care.

So it was news to me that there were six missing sections from our map. Pin-Lee and Gurathin had found the discrepancies and Mensah wanted to know if I thought it was just the survey package being cheap and error-ridden or if I thought this was part of a hack. I appreciated the fact that we were communicating via the feed and that she wasn't making me actually speak to her on the comm. I was so appreciative I gave her my real opinion, that it probably was the fact that our survey package was a cheap piece of crap but the only way to know for certain was to go out and look at one of the missing sections and see if there was anything there besides more boring planet. I didn't phrase it exactly like that but that was what I meant.

She took her attention off the feed then, but I stayed alert, since I knew she tended to make her decisions fast and if I started a show again I'd just get interrupted. I did check the security-camera view of the hub so I could hear their conversation. They all wanted to check it out, and were just going back and forth on whether they should wait. They had just had a comm conversation with Delt-Fall on the other continent who had agreed to send copies of the missing survey package files. Some of the clients wanted to see if anything else was missing first, and others wanted to go now, and *blah, blah, blah.*

I knew how this was going to turn out.

It wasn't a long trip, not far outside the range of the other assessments they had been doing, but not knowing what they were flying into was definitely a red flag for security. In a smart world, I should go alone, but with the governor module I had to be within a hundred meters of at least one of the clients at all times, or it would fry me. They knew that, so volunteering to take a solo cross-continental trip might set off a few alarms.

So when Mensah opened the feed again to tell me they were going, I told her security protocols suggested that I should go, too.

Chapter Three

WE GOT READY to leave at the beginning of the day cycle, in the morning light, and the satellite weather report said it would be a good day for flying and scanning. I checked MedSystem and saw Bharadwaj was awake and talking.

It wasn't until I was helping to carry equipment to the little hopper that I realized they were going to make me ride in the crew cabin.

At least I was in the armor with my helmet opaqued. But when Mensah told me to get in the copilot's seat, it didn't turn out to be as bad as my first horrified realization. Arada and Pin-Lee didn't try to talk to me, and Ratthi actually looked away when I eased past him to get to the cockpit.

They were all so careful not to look at me or talk to me directly that as soon as we were in the air I did a quick spot check through HubSystem's records of their conversations. I had talked myself into believing that I hadn't actually lost it as much as I thought I had when Mensah had offered to let me hang out in the hub with the humans like I was an actual person or something.

The conversation they had immediately after that gave me a sinking sensation as I reviewed it. No, it had been worse than I thought. They had talked it over and all agreed not to "push me any further than I wanted to go" and they were all so nice and it was just excruciating. I was never taking off the helmet again. I can't do even the half-assed version of this stupid job if I have to talk to humans.

They were the first clients I'd had who hadn't had any previous experience with SecUnits, so maybe I could have expected this if I'd bothered to think about it. Letting them see me without the armor had been a huge mistake.

At least Mensah and Arada had overruled the ones who wanted to talk to me about it. Yes, talk to Murderbot about its feelings. The idea was so painful I dropped to 97 percent efficiency. I'd rather climb back into Hostile One's mouth.

I worried about it while they looked out the windows at the ring or watched their feeds of the hopper's scans of the new scenery, chatting on the comm with the others who were following our progress back in the habitat. I was distracted, but still caught the moment when the autopilot cut out.

It could have been a problem, except I was in the

copilot's seat and I could have taken over in time. But even if I hadn't been there, it would have turned out okay, because Mensah was flying and she never took her hands off the controls.

Even though the planetary craft autopilots aren't as sophisticated as a full bot-pilot system, some clients will still engage it and then walk into the back, or sleep. Mensah didn't and she made sure when the others flew they followed her rules. She just made some thoughtful grumpy noises and adjusted our course away from the mountain the failing autopilot would have slammed us into.

I had cycled out of horrified that they wanted to talk to me about my feelings into grateful that she had ordered them not to. As she restarted the autopilot, I pulled the log and sent it into the feed to show her it had cut out due to a HubSystem glitch. She swore under her breath and shook her head.

———————

The missing map section wasn't that far outside our assessment range so we were there before I made a dent in the backlog of serials I'd saved to my internal storage. Mensah told the others, "We're coming up on it."

We had been traveling over heavy tropical forest,

where it flowed over deep valleys. Suddenly it dropped away into a plain, spotted with lakes and smaller copses of trees. There was a lot of bare rock, in low ridges and tumbled boulders. It was dark and glassy, like volcanic glass.

The cabin was quiet as everybody studied the scans. Arada was looking at the seismic data, bouncing it to the others back in the habitat through her feed.

"I don't see anything that would prevent the satellite from mapping this region," Pin-Lee said, her voice distant as she sorted through the data the hopper was pulling in. "No strange readings. It's weird."

"Unless this rock has some sort of stealth property that prevented the satellites from imaging it," Arada said. "The scanners are acting a little funny."

"Because the scanners suck corporation balls," Pin-Lee muttered.

"Should we land?" Mensah said. I realized she was asking me for a security assessment.

The scans were sort of working and marking some hazards, but they weren't any different hazards from what we'd run into before. I said, "We could. But we know there's at least one lifeform here that tunnels through rock."

Arada bounced a little in her seat, like she was impatient to get going. "I know we have to be cautious, but

I think we'd be safer if we knew whether these blank patches on the satellite scan were accidental or deliberate."

That was when I realized they weren't ignoring the possibility of sabotage. I should have realized it earlier, when Pin-Lee asked if HubSystem could be hacked. But humans had been looking at me and I had just wanted to get out of there.

Ratthi and Pin-Lee seconded her, and Mensah made her decision. "We'll land and take samples."

Over the comm from the habitat, Bharadwaj's voice said, "Please be careful." She still sounded shaky.

Mensah took us down gently, the hopper's pads touching the ground with hardly a thump. I was already up and at the hatch.

The humans had their suit helmets on so I opened the hatch and let the ramp drop. Close up the rocky patches still looked like glass, mostly black, but with different colors running into each other. This near to the ground the hopper's scan was able to confirm that seismic activity was null, but I walked out a little bit, as if giving anything out there a chance to attack me. If the humans see me actually doing my job, it helps keep suspicions from forming about faulty governor modules.

Mensah climbed down with Arada behind her. They moved around, taking more readings with their portable scanners. Then the others got the sample kit outs and started chipping off pieces of the rock glass, or glass rock, scooping up dirt and bits of plant matter. They were murmuring to each other a lot, and to the others back at the habitat. They were sending the data to the feed, but I wasn't paying attention.

It was an odd spot. Quiet compared to the other places we'd surveyed, with not much bird-thing noise and no sign of animal movement. Maybe the rocky patches kept them away. I walked out a little way, past a couple of the lakes, almost expecting to see something under the surface. Dead bodies, maybe. I'd seen plenty of those (and caused plenty of those) on past contracts, but this one had been dead-body-lacking, so far. It made for a nice change.

Mensah had set a survey perimeter, marking all the areas the aerial scan had flagged as hazardous or potentially hazardous. I checked on everybody again and saw Arada and Ratthi heading directly for one of the hazard markers. I expected them to stop at the perimeter, since they'd been pretty consistently cautious on the other assessments. I started moving in that direction anyway. Then they passed the perimeter. I started to run. I sent Mensah my field camera feed and used the voice comm to say, "Dr. Arada, Dr. Ratthi, please stop. You're past the perimeter and nearing a hazard marker."

"We are?" Ratthi sounded completely baffled.

Fortunately, they both stopped. By the time I got there they both had their maps up in my feed. "I don't understand what's wrong," Arada said, confused. "I don't see the hazard marker." She had tagged both their positions and on their maps they were well within the perimeter, heading toward a wetland area.

It took me a second to see what the problem was. Then I superimposed my map, the actual map, over theirs and sent that to Mensah. "Shit," she said over the comm. "Ratthi, Arada, your map's wrong. How did that happen?"

"It's a glitch," Ratthi said. He grimaced, studying the displays in his feed. "It's wiped out all the markers on this side."

So that was how I spent the rest of the morning, shooing humans away from hazard markers they couldn't see, while Pin-Lee cursed a lot and tried to get the mapping scanner to work. "I'm beginning to think these missing sections are just a mapping error," Ratthi said at one point, panting. He had walked into what they called a hot mud pit and I'd had to pull him out. We were both covered with acidic mud to the waist.

"You think?" Pin-Lee answered tiredly.

When Mensah told us to head back to the hopper, it was a relief all around.

We got back to the habitat with no problems, which felt like it was starting to become an unusual occurrence. The humans went to analyze their data, and I went to hide in the ready room, check the security feeds, and then lie in my cubicle and watch media for a while.

I'd just done another perimeter walk and checked the drones, when the feed informed me that HubSystem had updates from the satellite and there was a package for me. I have a trick where I make HubSystem think I received it and then just put it in external storage. I don't do automated package updates anymore, now that I don't have to. When I felt like it, presumably sometime before it was time to leave the planet, I'd go through the update and apply the parts I wanted and delete the rest.

It was a typical, boring day, in other words. If Bharadwaj wasn't still recuperating in Medical, you could almost forget what had happened. But at the end of the day cycle, Dr. Mensah called me again and said, "I think we have a problem. We can't contact DeltFall Group."

I went to the crew hub where Mensah and all the others were. They had pulled up the maps and scans of where we were versus where DeltFall was, and the curve of the planet hung glittering in the air in the big display. When I got there, Mensah was saying, "I've checked the big hopper's specs and we can make it there and back without a recharge."

I had my helmet plate opaqued, so I could wince a lot without any of them knowing.

"You don't think they'll let us recharge at their habitat?" Arada asked, then looked around when the others stared at her. "What?" she demanded.

Overse put an arm around her and squeezed her shoulder. "If they aren't answering our calls, they might be hurt, or their habitat is damaged," she said. As a couple, they were always so nice to each other. The whole group had been remarkably drama-free so far, which I appreciated. The last few contracts had been like being an involuntary bystander in one of the entertainment feed's multi-partner relationship serials except I'd hated the whole cast.

Mensah nodded. "That's my concern, especially if their survey package was missing potential hazard information the way ours is."

Arada looked like it was just occurring to her that everybody over at DeltFall might be dead.

Ratthi said, "The thing that worries me is that their emergency beacon didn't launch. If the habitat was breached, or if there was a medical emergency they couldn't handle, their HubSystem should have triggered the beacon automatically."

Each survey team has its own beacon, set up a safe distance from the habitat. It would launch into a low orbit and send a pulse toward the wormhole, which would get zapped or whatever happened in the wormhole and the company network would get it, and the pickup transport would be sent now instead of waiting until the end of project date. That was how it was supposed to work, anyway. Usually.

Mensah's expression said she was worried. She looked at me. "What do you think?"

It took me two seconds to realize she was talking to me. Fortunately, since it seemed like we were really doing this, I had actually been paying attention and didn't need to play the conversation back. I said, "They have three contracted SecUnits but if their habitat was hit by a hostile as big or bigger than Hostile One, their comm equipment could have been damaged."

Pin-Lee was calling up specs for the beacons. "Aren't the emergency beacons designed to trigger even if the rest of the comm equipment is destroyed?"

The other good thing about my hacked governor module is that I could ignore the governor's instructions to defend the stupid company. "They're supposed to be able to, but equipment failures aren't unknown."

There was a moment where they all thought about potential equipment failures in their habitat, maybe including the big hopper which they were about to fly out of range of the little hopper, so if something happened to it they were walking back. And swimming back, since that was an ocean-sized body of water between the two points on the map. Or drown; I guess they could just drown. If you were wondering why I was wincing earlier, this would be the reason.

The trip to the map's black-out region had been a little out of our assessment parameters, but this was going to be an overnight trip, even if all they did was get there, see a bunch of dead people, turn around and go back.

Then Gurathin said, "What about your systems?"

I didn't turn my helmet toward him because that can be intimidating and it's especially important for me to resist that urge. "I carefully monitor my own systems." What else did he think I was going to say? It didn't matter; I'm not refundable.

Volescu cleared his throat. "So we should prepare for a rescue mission." He looked okay, but MedSystem's feed was still reporting some indicators of distress. Bharadwaj was stable but not allowed to get out of Medical yet. He continued, "I've pulled some instructions from the hopper's info package."

Yes, instructions. They're academics, surveyors, researchers, not action-hero explorers from the serials I liked because they were unrealistic and not depressing and sordid like reality. I said, "Dr. Mensah, I think I should go along."

I could see her notes in the feed so I knew she meant for me to stay here and watch the habitat and guard everybody who wasn't going. She was taking Pin-Lee, because she had past experience in habitat and shelter construction; Ratthi, who was a biologist; and Overse, who was certified as a field medic.

Mensah hesitated, thinking about it, and I could tell she was debating protecting the habitat and the group staying behind with the possibility of whatever had hit DeltFall still being there. She took a breath and I knew she was going to tell me to stay here. And I just thought, *That's a bad idea.* I couldn't explain to myself why. It was one of those impulses that comes from my organic parts that the governor is supposed to squash. I said, "As the only one here with experience in these situations, I'm your best resource."

Gurathin said, "What situations?"

Ratthi gave him a bemused look. "This situation. The unknown. Strange threats. Monsters exploding out of the ground."

I was glad I wasn't the only one who thought it was a

dumb question. Gurathin wasn't as talkative as the others, so I didn't have much of a sense of his personality. He was the only augmented human in the group, so maybe he felt like an outsider, or something, even though the others clearly liked him. I clarified, "Situations where personnel might be injured due to attack by planetary hazards."

Arada came in on my side. "I agree. I think you should take SecUnit. You don't know what's out there."

Mensah was still undecided. "Depending on what we find, we may be gone as long as two or three days."

Arada waved a hand, indicating the habitat. "Nothing's bothered us here so far."

That was probably what DeltFall had thought, right before they got eaten or torn to pieces or whatever. But Volescu said, "I admit it would make me feel better about it." From Medical, Bharadwaj tapped into the feed to add her vote for me. Gurathin was the only one staying behind who didn't say anything.

Mensah nodded firmly. "All right then, it's decided. Now let's get moving."

So I prepped the big hopper to go to the other side of the planet. (And yes, I had to pull up the instructions.)

I checked it over as much as I could, remembering how the autopilot had cut out suddenly in the little hopper. But we hadn't used the big hopper since Mensah had taken it up to check it out when we arrived. (You had to check everything out and log any problems immediately when you took delivery or the company wasn't liable.) But everything looked okay, or at least matched what the specs said it was supposed to match. It was only there for emergencies and if this thing with DeltFall hadn't happened, we would probably never have touched it until it was time to lift it onto our pickup transport.

Mensah came to do her own check of the hopper, and told me to pack some extra emergency supplies for the DeltFall staff. I did it, and I hoped for the humans' sake we would need them. I thought it was likely that the only supplies we would need for DeltFall was the postmortem kind, but you may have noticed that when I do manage to care, I'm a pessimist.

When everything was ready, Overse, Ratthi, and Pin-Lee climbed in, and I stood hopefully by the cargo pod. Mensah pointed at the cabin. I winced behind my opaque faceplate and climbed in.

Chapter Four

WE FLEW THROUGH THE NIGHT, the humans taking scans and discussing the new terrain past our assessment range. It was especially interesting for them to see what was there, now that we knew our map wasn't exactly reliable.

Mensah gave everybody watch shifts, including me. This was new, but not unwelcome, as it meant I had blocks of time where I wasn't supposed to be paying attention and didn't have to fake it. Mensah, Pin-Lee, and Overse were all taking turns as pilot and copilot, so I didn't have to worry so much about the autopilot trying to kill us, and I could go on standby and watch my stored supply of serials.

We'd been in the air awhile, and Mensah was piloting with Pin-Lee in the copilot's seat, when Ratthi turned in his seat to face me and said, "We heard—we were given to understand, that Imitative Human Bot Units are ... partially constructed from cloned material."

Warily, I stopped the show I was watching. I didn't like where this might go. All of that information is in the common knowledge database, plus in the brochure the company provides with the specifics of the types of units they use. Which he knew, being a scientist and whatever. And he wasn't the kind of human who asked about things when he could look them up himself through a feed. "That's true," I said, very careful to make my voice sound just as neutral as always.

Ratthi's expression was troubled. "But surely . . . It's clear you have feelings—"

I flinched. I couldn't help it.

Overse had been working in the feed, analyzing data from the assessments. She looked up, frowning. "Ratthi, what are you doing?"

Ratthi shifted guiltily. "I know Mensah asked us not to, but—" He waved a hand. "You saw it."

Overse pulled her interface off. "You're upsetting it," she said, teeth gritted.

"That's my point!" He gestured in frustration. "The practice is disgusting, it's horrible, it's slavery. This is no more a machine than Gurathin is—"

Exasperated, Overse said, "And you don't think it knows that?"

I'm supposed to let the clients do and say whatever they want to me and with an intact governor module I wouldn't have a choice. I'm also not supposed to snitch on clients to anybody except the company, but it was either that or jump out the hatch. I sent the conversation into the feed tagged for Mensah.

From the cockpit, she shouted, "Ratthi! We talked about this!"

I slid out of the seat and went to the back of the hopper, as far away as I could get, facing the supply lockers and the head. It was a mistake; it wasn't a normal thing for a SecUnit with an intact governor module to do, but they didn't notice.

"I'll apologize," Ratthi was saying.

"No, just leave it alone," Mensah told him.

"That would just make it worse," Overse added.

I stood there until they all calmed down and got quiet again, then slid into a seat in the back, and resumed the serial I'd been watching.

It was the middle of the night when I felt the feed drop out.

I hadn't been using it, but I had the SecSystem feeds from the drones and the interior cameras backburnered and was accessing them occasionally to make sure everything was okay. The humans left behind in the habitat were more active than they usually were at this time, probably anxious about what we were going to find at

DeltFall. I was hearing Arada walk around occasionally, though Volescu was snoring off and on in his bunk. Bharadwaj had been able to move back to her own quarters, but was restless and going over her field notes through the feed. Gurathin was in the hub doing something on his personal system. I wondered what he was doing and had just started to carefully poke around through HubSystem to find out. When the feed dropped it was like someone slapped the organic part of my brain.

I sat up and said, "The satellite went down."

The others, except for Pin-Lee who was piloting, all grabbed for their interfaces. I saw their expressions when they felt the silence. Mensah pushed out of her seat and came to the back. "Are you sure it was the satellite?"

"I'm sure," I told her. "I'm pinging it and there's no response."

We still had our local feed, running on the hopper's system, so we could communicate through it as well as the comm and share data with each other. We just didn't have nearly as much data as we'd have had if we were still attached to HubSystem. We were far enough away that we needed the comm satellite as a relay. Ratthi switched his interface to the hopper's feed and started checking the scans. There was nothing on them except empty sky; I had them backburnered but I'd set them to notify me if they encountered anything like an energy reading or a large life sign. He said, "I just felt a chill. Did anyone else feel a chill?"

"A little," Overse admitted. "It's a weird coincidence, isn't it?"

"The damn satellite's had periodic outages since we got here," Pin-Lee pointed out from the cockpit. "We just don't normally need it for comms." She was right. I was supposed to check their personal logs periodically in case they were plotting to defraud the company or murder each other or something, and the last time I'd looked at Pin-Lee's she had been tracking the satellite problems, trying to figure out if there was a pattern. It was one of the many things I didn't care about because the entertainment feed was only updated occasionally, and I downloaded it for local storage.

Ratthi shook his head. "But this is the first time we've been far enough from the habitat to need it for comm contact. It just seems odd, and not in a good way."

Mensah looked around at them. "Does anyone want to turn back?"

I did, but I didn't get a vote. The others sat there for a quiet moment, then Overse said, "If it turns out the Delt-Fall group did need help, and we didn't go, how would we feel?"

"If there's a chance we can save lives, we have to take it," Pin-Lee agreed.

Ratthi sighed. "No, you're right. I'd feel terrible if any-one died because we were overcautious."

"We're agreed, then," Mensah said. "We'll keep going."

I would have preferred they be overcautious. I had had contracts before where the company's equipment glitched this badly, but there was just something about this that made me think it was more. But all I had was the feeling.

I had four hours to my next scheduled watch so I went into standby, and buried myself in the downloads I'd stored away.

———

It was dawn when we got there. DeltFall had established their camp in a wide valley surrounded by high moun-tains. A spiderweb of creek beds cut through the grass and stubby trees. They were a bigger operation than ours, with three linked habitats, and a shelter for surface ve-hicles, plus a landing area for two large hoppers, a cargo hauler, and three small hoppers. It was all company equipment though, per contract, and all subject to the same malfunctions as the crap they'd dumped on us.

There was no one outside, no movement. No sign of damage, no sign any hostile fauna had approached. The satellite was still dead, but Mensah had been trying to get the DeltFall habitat on the comm since we had come within range.

"Are they missing any transports?" Mensah asked.

Ratthi checked the record of what they were supposed to have which I'd copied from HubSystem before we left. "No, the hoppers are all there. Their ground vehicles are in that shelter, I think."

I had moved up to the front as we got closer. Standing behind the pilot's seat, I said, "Dr. Mensah, I recommend you land outside their perimeter." Through the local feed I sent her all the info I had, which was that their automated systems were responding to the pings the hopper was sending, but that was it. We weren't picking up their feed, which meant their HubSystem was in standby. There was nothing from their three SecUnits, not even pings.

Overse, in the copilot's seat, glanced up at me. "Why?"

I had to answer the question so I said, "Security protocol," which sounded good and didn't commit me to anything. No one outside, no one answering the comm. Unless they had all jumped in their surface vehicles and gone off on vacation, leaving their Hub and SecUnits shut down, they were dead. Pessimism confirmed.

But we couldn't be sure without looking. The hopper's scanners can't see inside the habitats because of the shielding that's really only there to protect proprietary data, so we couldn't get any life signs or energy readings.

This is why I didn't want to come. I've got four per-fectly good humans here and I didn't want them to get killed by whatever took out DeltFall. It's not like I cared about them personally, but it would look bad on my record, and my record was already pretty terrible.

"We're just being cautious," Mensah said, answering Overse. She took the hopper down at the edge of the val-ley, on the far side of the streams.

I gave Mensah a few hints through the feed, that they should break out the handweapons in the survival gear, that Ratthi should stay behind inside the hopper with the hatch sealed and locked since he'd never done the weapon-training course, and that, most important, I should go first. They were quiet, subdued. Up until now, I think they had all been looking at this as probably a nat-ural disaster, that they were going to be digging survivors out of a collapsed habitat, or helping fight off a herd of Hostile Ones.

This was something else.

Mensah gave the orders and we started forward, me in front, the humans a few steps behind. They were in their full suits with helmets, which gave some protection but had been meant for environmental hazards, not some other heavily armed human (or angry malfunctioning rogue SecUnit) deliberately trying to kill them. I was more nervous than Ratthi, who was jittery on our comms, monitoring the scans, and basically telling us to be careful every other step.

I had my built-in energy weapons and the big projectile weapon I was cradling. I also had six drones, pulled from the hopper's supply and under my control through its feed. They were the small kind, barely a centimeter across; no weapons, just cameras. (They make some which aren't much bigger and have a small pulse weapon, but you have to get one of the upper-tier company packages mostly designed for much larger contracts.) I told the drones to get in the air and gave them a scouting pattern.

I did that because it seemed sensible, not because I knew what I was doing. I am not a combat murderbot, I'm Security. I keep things from attacking the clients and try to gently discourage the clients from attacking each other. I was way out of my depth here, which was another reason I hadn't wanted the humans to come here.

We crossed the shallow streams, sending a group of water invertebrates scattering away from our boots. The trees were short and sparse enough that I had a good view of the camp from this angle. I couldn't detect any DeltFall security drones, by eye or with the scanners on my drones. Ratthi in the hopper wasn't picking up anything either. I really, really wished I could pinpoint the location of those three SecUnits, but I wasn't getting anything from them.

SecUnits aren't sentimental about each other. We aren't friends, the way the characters on the serials are, or the way my humans were. We can't trust each other, even if we work together. Even if you don't have clients who decide to entertain themselves by ordering their SecUnits to fight each other.

The scans read the perimeter sensors as dead and the drones weren't picking up any warning indicators. The DeltFall HubSystem was down, and without it, no one inside could access our feed or comms, theoretically. We crossed over and into the landing area for their hoppers. They were between us and the first habitat, the vehicle storage to one side. I was leading us in at an angle, trying to get a visual on the main habitat door, but I was also checking the ground. It was mostly bare of grass from all the foot traffic and hopper landings. From the weather report we'd gotten before the satellite quit, it had rained here last night, and the mud had hardened. No activity since then.

I passed that info to Mensah through the feed and she told the others. Keeping her voice low, Pin-Lee said, "So whatever happened, it wasn't long after we spoke to them on the comm."

"They couldn't have been attacked by someone,"

Overse whispered. There was no reason to whisper, but I understood the impulse. "There's no one else on this planet."

"There's not supposed to be anyone else on this planet," Ratthi said, darkly, over the comm from our hopper.

There were three SecUnits who were not me on this planet, and that was dangerous enough. I got my visual on the main habitat hatch and saw it was shut, no sign of anything forcing its way inside. The drones had circled the whole structure by now, and showed me the other entrances were the same. That was that. Hostile Fauna don't come to the door and ask to be let inside. I sent the images to Mensah's feed and said aloud, "Dr. Mensah, it would be better if I went ahead."

She hesitated, reviewing what I'd just sent her. I saw her shoulders tense. I think she had just come to the same conclusion I had. Or at least admitted to herself that it was the strongest possibility. She said, "All right. We'll wait here. Make sure we can monitor."

She'd said "we" and she wouldn't have said that if she didn't mean it, unlike some clients I'd had. I sent my field camera's feed to all four of them and started forward.

I called four of the drones back, leaving two to keep circling the perimeter. I checked the vehicle shed as I moved past it. It was open on one side, with some sealed lockers in the back for storage. All four of their surface vehicles were there, powered down, no sign of recent tracks, so I didn't go in. I wouldn't bother searching the small storage spaces until we got down to the looking-for-all-the-body-parts phase.

I walked up to the hatch of the first habitat. We didn't have an entry code, so I was expecting to have to blow the door, but when I tapped the button it slid open for me. I told Mensah through the feed that I wouldn't speak aloud on the comm anymore.

She tapped back an acknowledgment on the feed, and I heard her telling the others to get off my feed and my comm, that she was going to be the only one speaking to me so I wasn't distracted. Mensah underestimated my ability to ignore humans but I appreciated the thought. Ratthi whispered, "Be careful," and signed off.

I had the weapon up going in, through the suit locker area and into the first corridor. "No suits missing," Mensah said in my ear, watching the field camera. I sent my four drones ahead, maintaining an interior scouting pattern. This was a nicer habitat than ours, wider halls, newer. Also empty, silent, the smell of decaying flesh drifting through my helmet filters. I headed toward the hub, where their main crew area should be.

The lights were still on and air whispered through the vents, but I couldn't get into their SecSystem with their feed down. I missed my cameras.

At the door to the hub, I found their first SecUnit. It was sprawled on its back on the floor, the armor over its chest pierced by something that made a hole approximately ten centimeters wide and a little deeper. We're hard to kill, but that'll do it. I did a brief scan to make sure it was inert, then stepped over it and went through into the crew area.

There were eleven messily dead humans in the hub, sprawled on the floor, in chairs, the monitoring stations and projection surfaces behind them showing impact damage from projectile and energy weapon fire. I tapped the feed and asked Mensah to fall back to the hopper. She acknowledged me and I got confirmation from my outside drones that the humans were retreating.

I went out the opposite door to a corridor that led toward the mess hall, Medical, and cabins. The drones were telling me the layout was very similar to our habitat, except for the occasional dead person sprawled in the corridors. The weapon that had taken out the dead SecUnit wasn't in the hub, and it had died with its back to the door. The DeltFall humans had had some warning, enough to start getting up and heading for the other exits, but something else had come in from this direction and trapped them. I thought that SecUnit had been killed trying to protect the hub.

Which meant I was looking for the other two SecUnits.

Maybe these clients had been terrible and abusive, maybe they had deserved it. I didn't care. Nobody was touching my humans. To make sure of that I had to kill these two rogue Units. I could have pulled out at this point, sabotaged the hoppers, and got my humans out of there, leaving the rogue Units stuck on the other side of an ocean; that would have been the smart thing to do.

But I wanted to kill them.

One of my drones found two humans dead in the mess, no warning. They had been taking food pacs out of the heating cubby, getting the tables ready for a meal.

While I moved through the corridors and rooms, I was doing an image search against the hopper's equipment database. The dead unit had probably been killed by a mineral survey tool, like a pressure or sonic drill. We had one on the hopper, part of the standard equipment. You would have to get close to use it with enough force to pierce armor, maybe a little more than a meter.

Because you can't walk up to another murderbot with an armor-piercing projectile or energy weapon inside the habitat and not be looked at with suspicion. You can walk up to a fellow murderbot with a tool that a human might have asked you to get.

By the time I reached the other side of the structure,

the drones had cleared the first habitat. I stood in the hatchway at the top of the narrow corridor that led into the second. A human lay at the opposite end, half in and half out of the open hatch. To get into the next habitat, I'd have to step over her to push the door all the way open. I could tell already that something was wrong about the body position. I used the magnification on the field camera to get a closer view of the skin on the outstretched arm. The lividity was wrong; she had been shot in the chest or face and lay on her back for some time, then had been moved here recently. Probably as soon as they picked up our hopper on the way here.

On the feed I told Mensah what I needed her to do. She didn't ask questions. She'd been watching my field camera, and she knew by now what we were dealing with. She tapped back to acknowledge me, then said aloud on the comm, "SecUnit, I want you to hold your position until I get there."

I said, "Yes, Dr. Mensah," and eased back out of the hatch. I moved fast, back to the security ready room.

It was nice having a human smart enough to work with like this.

Our model of habitat didn't have it but on these bigger ones there's a roof access and my outside drones had a good view of it.

I climbed the ladder up to the roof hatch and popped

it. The armor's boots have magnetized climbing clamps, and I used them to cross over the curving roofs to the third habitat and then around to the second, coming up on them from behind. Even these two rogues wouldn't be dumb enough to ignore the creaks if I took the quick route and walked over to their position.

(They were not the sharpest murderbots, having cleaned the floor of the between-habitat corridor to cover the prints they had left when staging that body. It would have fooled somebody who hadn't noticed all the other floors were covered with tracked-in dust.)

I opened the roof access for the second habitat and sent my drones ahead down into the Security ready room. Once they checked the unit cubicles and made sure nobody was home, I dropped down the ladder. A lot of their equipment was still there, including their drones. There was a nice box of new ones, but they were useless without the DeltFall HubSystem. Either it was really dead or doing a good imitation of it. I still kept part of my attention on it; if it came up suddenly and reactivated the security cameras, the rules of the game would change abruptly.

Keeping my drones with me, I took the inner corridor and moved silently past Medical's blasted hatch. Three bodies were piled inside where the humans had tried to secure it and been trapped when their own SecUnits blew it open to slaughter them.

When I was close to the corridor with the hatch where both units were waiting for me and Dr. Mensah to come wandering in, I sent the drones around for a careful look. Oh yeah, there they were.

With no weapons on my drones, the only way to do this was to move fast. So I threw myself around the last corner, hit the opposite wall, crossed back and kept going, firing at their positions.

I hit the first one with three explosive bolts in the back and one in the faceplate as it turned toward me. It dropped. The other one I nicked in the arm, taking out the joint, and it made the mistake of switching its main weapon to its other hand, which gave me a couple of seconds. I switched to rapid fire to keep it off balance, then back to the explosive bolt. That dropped it.

I hit the floor, needing a minute to recover.

I had taken at least a dozen hits from both of their energy weapons while I was taking out the first one, but the explosive bolts had missed me, going past to tear up the corridor. Even with the armor, bits of me were going numb, but I had only taken three projectiles to the right shoulder, four to the left hip. This is how we fight: throw ourselves at each other and see whose parts give out first.

Neither unit was dead. But they were incapable of reaching their cubicles in the ready room, and I sure as hell wasn't going to give them a hand.

Three of my drones were down, too; they had gone into combat mode and slammed in ahead of me to draw fire. One had gotten hit by a stray energy burst and was wandering around in the corridor behind me. I checked my two perimeter drones by habit, and opened my comm to Dr. Mensah to tell her I still needed to clear the rest of the habitat and do the formal check for survivors.

The drone behind me went out with a fizzle that I heard and saw on the feed. I think I realized immediately what that meant but there may have been a half second or so of delay. But I was on my feet when something hit me so hard I was suddenly on my back on the floor, systems failing.

I came back online to no vision, no hearing, no ability to move. I couldn't reach the feed or the comm. Not good, Murderbot, not good.

I suddenly got some weird flashes of sensation, all from my organic parts. Air on my face, my arms, through rips in my suit. On the burning wound in my shoulder. Someone had taken off my helmet and the upper part of my armor. The sensations were only for seconds at a time. It was confusing and I wanted to scream. Maybe this was how murderbots died. You lose function, go offline, but parts of you keep working, organic pieces kept alive by the fading energy in your power cells.

Then I knew someone was moving me, and I really wanted to scream.

I fought back panic, and got a few more flashes of sensation. I wasn't dead. I was in a lot of trouble.

I waited to get some kind of function back, frantic, disoriented, terrified, wondering why they hadn't blown a hole in my chest. Sound came first, and I knew something leaned over me. Faint noises from the joints told me it was a SecUnit. But there'd only been three. I'd checked the DeltFall specs before we left. I do a half-assed job sometimes, okay, most of the time, but Pin-Lee had checked, too, and she was thorough.

Then my organic parts started to sting, the numbness wearing off. I was designed to work with both organic and machine parts, to balance that sensory input. Without the balance, I felt like a balloon floating in mid-air. But the organic part of my chest was in contact with a hard surface, and that abruptly brought my position into focus. I was lying face down, one arm dangling. They'd put me on a table?

This was definitely not good.

Pressure on my back, then on my head. The rest of me was coming back but slowly, slowly. I felt for the feed but couldn't reach it. Then something stabbed me in the back of the neck.

That's organic material and with the rest of me down there was nothing to control input from my nervous system. It felt like they were sawing my head off.

A shock went through me and suddenly the rest of me was back online. I popped the joint on my left arm so I could move it in a way not usually compatible with a human, augmented human, or murderbot body. I reached up to the pressure and pain on my neck, and grabbed an armored wrist. I twisted my whole body and took us both off the table.

We hit the floor and I clamped my legs around the other SecUnit as we rolled. It tried to trigger the weapons built into its forearm but my reaction speed was off the chart and I clamped a hand over the port so it couldn't open fully. My vision was back and I could see its opaqued helmet inches away. My armor had been removed down to my waist, and that just made me more angry.

I shoved its hand up under its chin and took the pressure off its weapon. It had a split second to try to abort that fire command and it failed. The energy burst went through my hand and the join between its helmet and neck piece. Its head jerked and its body started to spasm. I let go of it long enough to kneel up, get my intact arm around its neck, and twist.

I let go as I felt the connections, mechanical and organic, snap.

I looked up and another SecUnit was in the doorway, lifting a large projectile weapon.

How many of these damn things were here? It didn't matter, because I tried to shove myself upright but I couldn't react fast enough. Then it jerked, dropped the weapon, and fell forward. I saw two things: the ten-centimeter hole in its back and Mensah standing behind it, holding something that looked a lot like the sonic mining drill from our hopper.

"Dr. Mensah," I said, "this is a violation of security priority and I am contractually obligated to record this for report to the company—" It was in the buffer and the rest of my brain was empty.

She ignored me, talking to Pin-Lee on the comm, and strode forward to grab my arm and pull. I was too heavy for her so I shoved upright so she wouldn't hurt herself. It was starting to occur to me that Dr. Mensah might actually be an intrepid galactic explorer, even if she didn't look like the ones on the entertainment feed.

She kept pulling on me so I kept moving. Something was wrong with one of my hip joints. Oh, right, I got shot there. Blood ran down my torn suit skin and I reached up to my neck. I expected to feel a gaping hole, but there was something stuck there. "Dr. Mensah, there might be more rogue units, we don't know—"

"That's why we need to hurry," she said, dragging me along. She had brought the last two drones with her from outside, but they were uselessly circling her head. Humans don't have enough access to the feed to control them and do other things, like walk and talk. I tried to reach them but I still couldn't get a clear link to the hopper's feed.

We turned into another corridor and Overse waited in the outer hatch. She hit the open panel as soon as she saw us. She had her handweapon out and I had time to notice that Mensah had my weapon under her other arm. "Dr. Mensah, I need my weapon."

"You're missing a hand and part of your shoulder," she snapped. Overse grabbed a handful of my suit skin and helped pull me out of the hatch. Dust swirled in the air as the hopper set down two meters away, barely clearing the habitat's extendable roof.

"Yeah, I know, but—" The hatch opened and Ratthi ducked out, grabbed the collar of my suit skin, and pulled all three of us up into the cabin.

I collapsed on the deck as we lifted off. I needed to do something about the hip joint. I tried to check the scan to make sure nobody was on the ground shooting at us but even here my connection to the hopper's system was twitchy, glitching so much I couldn't see any reports from the instrumentation, like something was blocking the . . .

Uh-oh.

I felt the back of my neck again. The larger part of the obstruction was gone, but I could feel something in the port now. My data port.

The DeltFall SecUnits hadn't been rogues, they had been inserted with combat override modules. The modules allow personal control over a SecUnit, turn it from a mostly autonomous construct into a gun puppet. The feed would be cut off, control would be over the comm, but functionality would depend on how complex the orders were. "Kill the humans" isn't a complex order.

Mensah stood over me, Ratthi leaned across a seat to look out toward the DeltFall camp, Overse popped open one of the storage lockers. They were talking, but I couldn't catch it. I sat up and said, "Mensah, you need to shut me down now."

"What?" She looked down at me. "We're getting—emergency repair—"

Sound was breaking up. It was the download flooding my system, and my organic parts weren't used to processing that much information. "The unknown SecUnit inserted a data carrier, a combat-override module. It's downloading instructions into me and will override my system. This is why the two DeltFall units turned rogue.

You have to stop me." I don't know why I was dancing around the word. Maybe because I thought she didn't want to hear it. She'd just shot a heavily armed SecUnit with a mining drill to get me back; presumably she wanted to keep me. "You have to kill me."

It took forever for them to realize what I'd said, put it together with what they must have seen on my field camera feed, but my ability to measure time was glitching, too.

"No," Ratthi said, looking down at me, horrified. "No, we can't—"

Mensah said, "We won't. Pin-Lee—"

Overse dropped the repair kit and climbed over two rows of seats, yelling for Pin-Lee. I knew she was going to the cockpit to take the controls so Pin-Lee could work on me. I knew she wouldn't have time to fix me. I knew I could kill everyone on the hopper, even with a blown hip joint and one working arm.

So I grabbed the handweapon lying on the seat, turned it toward my chest, and pulled the trigger.

```
performance reliability at 10% and dropping
            shutdown initiated
```

Chapter Five

I CAME BACK ONLINE to find I was inert, but slowly cycling into a wake-up phase. I was agitated, my levels were all off, and I had no idea why. I played back my personal log. Oh, right.

I shouldn't be waking up. I hoped they hadn't been stupid about it, too soft-hearted to kill me.

You notice I didn't point the weapon at my head. I didn't want to kill myself, but it was going to have to be done. I could have incapacitated myself some other way, but let's face it, I didn't want to sit around and listen to the part where they convinced each other that there was no other choice.

A diagnostic initiated and informed me the combat override module had been removed. For a second I didn't believe it. I opened my security feed and found a camera for Medical. I was lying on the procedure table, my armor gone, just wearing what was left of my suit skin, the humans gathered around. That was a bit of a nightmare image. But my shoulder, hand, and hip had been repaired, so I'd been in my cubicle at some point. I ran the recording back a little and watched Pin-Lee and Overse use the surgical suite to deftly remove the combat module from the back of my head. It was such a relief, I played the recording twice, then ran a diagnostic. My logs were clear; nothing there except what I'd had before entering the DeltFall habitat.

My clients are the best clients.

Then hearing came online.

"I've had HubSystem immobilize it," Gurathin said.

Huh. Well, that explained a lot. I still had control of SecSystem and I told it to freeze HubSystem's access to its feed and implement my emergency routine. This was a function I'd built in that would substitute an hour or so of ambient habitat noise in place of the visual and audio recordings HubSystem made. To anyone listening to us through HubSystem, or trying to play back the recording, it would just sound like everybody had abruptly stopped talking.

What Gurathin had said had evidently been a surprise, because voices protested, Ratthi, Volescu, and Arada mostly. Pin-Lee was saying impatiently, "There's no danger. When it shot itself, it froze the download. I was able to remove the few fragments of rogue code that had been copied over."

Overse began, "Do you want to do your own diagnostic, because—"

I could hear them in the room and on the security feed, so I switched to just visual on the camera. Mensah had held up a hand for quiet. She said, "Gurathin, what's wrong?"

Gurathin said, "With it offline, I was able to use Hub-System to get some access to its internal system and log. I wanted to explore some anomalies I'd noticed through the feed." He gestured to me. "This unit was already a rogue. It has a hacked governor module."

On the entertainment feed, this is what they call an "oh shit" moment.

Through the security cams, I watched them be confused, but not alarmed, not yet.

Pin-Lee, who had apparently just been digging around in my local system, folded her arms. Her expression was sharp and skeptical. "I find that difficult to believe." She didn't add "you asshole" but it was in her voice. She didn't like anybody questioning her expertise.

"It doesn't have to follow our commands; there is no control over its behavior," Gurathin said, getting impatient. He didn't like anybody questioning his expertise either, but he didn't show it like Pin-Lee did. "I showed Volescu my evaluations and he agrees with me."

I had a moment to feel betrayed, which was stupid. Volescu was my client, and I'd saved his life because that was my job, not because I liked him. But then Volescu said, "I don't agree with you."

"The governor module is working, then?" Mensah asked, frowning at all of them.

"No, it's definitely hacked," Volescu explained. When he wasn't being attacked by giant fauna, he was a pretty calm guy. "The governor's connection to the rest of the SecUnit's system is partially severed. It can transmit commands, but can't enforce them or control behavior or apply punishment. But I think the fact that the Unit has been acting to preserve our lives, to take care of us, while it was a free agent, gives us even more reason to trust it."

Okay, so I did like him.

Gurathin insisted, "We've been sabotaged since we got here. The missing hazard report, the missing map sections. The SecUnit must be part of that. It's acting for the company, they don't want this planet surveyed for whatever reason. This is what must have happened to DeltFall."

Ratthi had been waiting for a moment to lunge in and interrupt. "Something odd is definitely going on. There were only three SecUnits for DeltFall in their specs, but there were five units in their habitat. Someone is sabotaging us, but I don't think our SecUnit is part of it."

With finality, Bharadwaj said, "Volescu and Ratthi are right. If the company did order the SecUnit to kill us, we would all be dead."

Overse sounded mad. "It told us about the combat module, it told us to kill it. Why the hell would it do that if it wanted to hurt us?"

I liked her, too. And even though being part of this conversation was the last thing I wanted to do, it was time to speak for myself.

I kept my eyes closed, watching them through the security camera, because that was easier. I made myself say, "The company isn't trying to kill you."

That startled them. Gurathin started to speak, and Pin-Lee shushed him. Mensah stepped forward, watching me with a worried expression. She was standing near me, with Gurathin and the others gathered in a loose circle around her. Bharadwaj was farthest back, sitting in a chair. Mensah said, "SecUnit, how do you know that?"

Even through the camera, this was hard. I tried to pretend I was back in my cubicle. "Because if the company wanted to sabotage you, they would have poisoned your supplies using the recycling systems. The company is more likely to kill you by accident."

There was a moment while they all thought about how easy it would have been for the company to sabotage its own environmental settings. Ratthi began, "But surely that would—"

Gurathin's expression was stiffer than usual. "This Unit has killed people before, people it was charged with pro-

tecting. It killed fifty-seven members of a mining operation."

What I told you before, about how I hacked my governor module but didn't become a mass murderer? That
was only sort of true. I was already a mass murderer.

I didn't want to explain. I had to explain. I said, "I did not
hack my governor module to kill my clients. My governor
module malfunctioned because the stupid company only
buys the cheapest possible components. It malfunctioned
and I lost control of my systems and I killed them. The company retrieved me and installed a new governor module. I
hacked it so it wouldn't happen again."

I think that's what happened. The only thing I know
for certain is that it didn't happen after I hacked the module. And it makes a better story that way. I watch enough
serials to know how a story like that should go.

Volescu looked sad. He shrugged a little. "My viewing
of the Unit's personal log that Gurathin obtained confirms that."

Gurathin turned to him, impatient. "The log confirms
it because that's what the Unit believes happened."

Bharadwaj sighed. "Yet here I sit, alive."

The silence was worse this time. On the feed I saw
Pin-Lee move uncertainly, glance at Overse and Arada.
Ratthi rubbed his face. Then Mensah said quietly,
"SecUnit, do you have a name?"

I wasn't sure what she wanted. "No."

"It calls itself 'Murderbot,'" Gurathin said.

I opened my eyes and looked at him; I couldn't stop myself. From their expressions I knew everything I felt was showing on my face, and I hate that. I grated out, "That was private."

The silence was longer this time.

Then Volescu said, "Gurathin, you wanted to know how it spends its time. That was what you were originally looking for in the logs. Tell them."

Mensah lifted her brows. "Well?"

Gurathin hesitated. "It's downloaded seven hundred hours of entertainment programming since we landed. Mostly serials. Mostly something called *Sanctuary Moon*." He shook his head, dismissing it. "It's probably using it to encode data for the company. It can't be watching it, not in that volume; we'd notice."

I snorted. He underestimated me.

Ratthi said, "The one where the colony's solicitor killed the terraforming supervisor who was the secondary donor for her implanted baby?"

Again, I couldn't help it. I said, "She didn't kill him, that's a fucking lie."

Ratthi turned to Mensah. "It's watching it."

Her expression fascinated, Pin-Lee asked, "But how did you hack your own governor module?"

"All the company equipment is the same." I got a download once that included all the specs for company systems. Stuck in a cubicle with nothing to do, I used it to work out the codes for the governor module.

Gurathin looked stubborn, but didn't say anything. I figured that was all he had, now it was my turn. I said, "You're wrong. HubSystem let you read my log, it let you find out about the hacked governor module. This is part of the sabotage. It wants you to stop trusting me because I'm trying to keep you alive."

Gurathin said, "We don't have to trust you. We just have to keep you immobilized."

Right, funny thing about that. "That won't work."

"And why is that?"

I rolled off the table, grabbed Gurathin by the throat and pinned him to the wall. It was fast, too fast for them to react. I gave them a second to realize what had happened, to gasp, and for Volescu to make a little *eek* noise. I said, "Because HubSystem lied to you when it told you I was immobilized."

Gurathin was red, but not as red as he would have been if I'd started applying pressure. Before anyone else could move, Mensah said, calm and even, "SecUnit, I'd appreciate it if you put Gurathin down, please."

She's a really good commander. I'm going to hack her file and put that in. If she'd gotten angry, shouted, let the others panic, I don't know what would have happened.

I told Gurathin, "I don't like you. But I like the rest of them, and for some reason I don't understand, they like you." Then I put him down.

I stepped away. Overse started toward him and Volescu grabbed his shoulder, but Gurathin waved them off. I hadn't even left a mark on his neck.

I was still watching them through the camera, because it was easier than looking directly at them. My suit skin was torn, revealing some of the joins in my organic and inorganic parts. I hate that. Everyone was still frozen, shocked, uncertain. Then Mensah took a sharp breath. She said, "SecUnit, can you keep HubSystem from accessing the security recordings from this room?"

I looked at the wall next to her head. "I cut it off when Gurathin said he found out my governor module was hacked, then deleted that section. I have the visual and audio recording transfer from SecSystem to HubSystem on a five-second delay."

"Good." Mensah nodded. She was trying to make eye contact but I couldn't do it right now. "Without the governor module, you don't have to obey our orders, or anybody's orders. But that's been the case the entire time we've been here."

The others were quiet, and I realized she was saying it for their benefit as much as mine.

She continued, "I would like you to remain part of our group, at least until we get off this planet and back to a place of safety. At that point, we can discuss what you'd like to do. But I swear to you, I won't tell the company, or anyone outside this room, anything about you or the broken module."

I sighed, managed to keep most of it internal. Of course she had to say that. What else could she do. I tried to decide whether to believe it or not, or whether it mattered, when I was hit by a wave of *I don't care*. And I really didn't. I said, "Okay."

In the camera feed, Ratthi and Pin-Lee exchanged a look. Gurathin grimaced, radiating skepticism. Mensah just said, "Is there any chance HubSystem knows about your governor module?"

I hated to admit this but they needed to know. Hacking myself is one thing, but I had hacked other systems, and I didn't know how they were going to react to that. "It might. I hacked HubSystem when we first arrived so it wouldn't notice that the commands sent to the governor module weren't always being followed, but if Hub-System's been compromised by an outside agent, I don't know if that worked. But HubSystem won't know you know about it."

Ratthi crossed his arms, his shoulders hunching uneasily. "We have to shut it down, or it's going to kill us."

Then he winced and looked at me. "Sorry, I meant Hub-System."

"No offense," I said.

"So we think HubSystem has been compromised by an outside agent," Bharadwaj said slowly, as if trying to convince herself. "Can we be certain it's not the company?"

I said, "Was DeltFall's beacon triggered?"

Mensah frowned, and Ratthi looked thoughtful again. He said, "We checked it on the way back, once we had you stabilized. It had been destroyed. So there was no reason for the attackers to do that if the company was their ally."

Everyone stood there, quiet. I could tell from their expressions they were all thinking hard. The HubSystem that controlled their habitat, that they were dependent on for food, shelter, filtered air, and water, was trying to kill them. And in their corner all they had was Murderbot, who just wanted everyone to shut up and leave it alone so it could watch the entertainment feed all day.

Then Arada came up and patted my shoulder. "I'm sorry. This must be very upsetting. After what that other Unit did to you . . . Are you all right?"

That was too much attention. I turned around and walked into the corner, facing away from them. I said, "There were two other instances of attempted sabotage

I'm aware of. When Hostile One attacked Drs. Bharadwaj and Volescu and I went to render assistance, I received an abort command from HubSystem through my governor module. I thought it was a glitch, caused by the MedSystem emergency feed trying to override HubSystem. When Dr. Mensah was flying the little hopper to check out the nearest map anomaly, the autopilot cut out just as we were crossing over a mountain range." I think that was it. Oh, right. "HubSystem downloaded an upgrade packet for me from the satellite before we left for DeltFall. I didn't apply it. You should probably look at what it would have told me to do."

Mensah said, "Pin-Lee, Gurathin, can you shut HubSystem down without compromising the environmental systems? And trigger our beacon without it interfering?"

Pin-Lee glanced at Gurathin and nodded. "It depends on what kind of condition you expect it to be in after we're done."

Mensah said, "Let's say don't blow it up, but you don't need to be gentle, either."

Pin-Lee nodded. "We can do that."

Gurathin cleared his throat. "It's going to know what we're doing. But if it doesn't have any instructions to stop us if we try, it may do nothing."

Bharadwaj leaned forward, frowning. "It's got to be reporting to someone. If it has a chance to warn them that we're shutting it down, they could supply instructions."

"We have to try it," Mensah said. She nodded to them. "Get moving."

Pin-Lee started for the door, but Gurathin said to Mensah, "Will you be all right here?"

He meant would they be all right with me here. I rolled my eyes.

"We'll be fine," Mensah said, firmly, with just a touch of *I said now*.

I watched him with the security cameras as he and Pin-Lee left, just in case he tried anything.

Volescu stirred. "We also need to look at that download from the satellite. Knowing what they wanted SecUnit to do might tell us a great deal."

Bharadwaj pushed herself up, a little unsteadily. "MedSystem is isolated from HubSystem, correct? That's why it hasn't been having failures. You could use it to unpack the download."

Volescu took her arm and they moved into the next cabin to the display surface there.

There was a little silence. The others could still listen to us on the feed, but at least they weren't in the room, and I felt the tension in my back and shoulders relax. It was easier to think. I was glad Mensah had told them to trigger our emergency beacon. Even if some of them were still suspicious of the company, it wasn't like there was another way off this planet.

Arada reached over and took Overse's hand. She said, "If it isn't the company that's doing this, who is it?"

"There has to be someone else here." Mensah rubbed her forehead, wincing as she thought. "Those two extra SecUnits at DeltFall came from somewhere. SecUnit, I'm assuming the company could be bribed to conceal the existence of a third survey team on this planet."

I said, "The company could be bribed to conceal the existence of several hundred survey teams on this planet." Survey teams, whole cities, lost colonies, traveling circuses, as long as they thought they could get away with it. I just didn't see how they could get away with making a client survey team—two client survey teams—vanish. Or why they'd want to. There were too many bond companies out there, too many competitors. Dead clients were terrible for business. "I don't think the company would collude with one set of clients to kill two other sets of clients. You purchased a bond agreement that the company would guarantee your safety or pay compensation in the event of your death or injury. Even if the company couldn't be held liable or partially liable for your deaths, they would still have to make the payment to your heirs. DeltFall was a large operation. The death payout for them alone will be huge." And the company hated to spend money. You could tell that by looking at the recycled upholstery on the habitat's furniture. "And if everyone believes the clients were killed by faulty SecUnits, the payment would be even bigger once all the lawsuits were filed."

On the cameras I could see nods and thoughtful expressions as they took that in. And they remembered that I had experience in what happened after SecUnits malfunctioned and killed clients.

"So the company took a bribe to conceal this third survey group, but not to let them kill us," Overse said. One of the good things about scientist clients is that they're quick on the uptake. "That means we just need to stay alive long enough for the pick-up transport to get here."

"But who is it?" Arada waved her hands. "We know whoever it is must have hacked control of the satellite." In the security camera, I saw her look toward me. "Is that how they took control of the DeltFall SecUnits? Through a download?"

It was a good question. I said, "It's possible. But it doesn't explain why one of the three DeltFall Units was killed outside the hub with a mining drill." We weren't supposed to be able to refuse a download, and I doubted there were other SecUnits hiding hacked governor modules. "If the DeltFall group refused the download for their SecUnits because they were experiencing the same increase in equipment failure that we were, the two unidentified Units could have been sent to manually infect the DeltFall Units."

Ratthi was staring into the distance, and through the feed I saw he was reviewing my field camera video of the DeltFall habitat. He pointed in my direction, nodding. "I agree, but it would mean the DeltFall group allowed the unknown Units into their habitat."

It was likely. We had checked to make sure all their hoppers were there, but it had been impossible to tell if an extra one had landed and taken off again at some point. Speaking of which, I did a quick check of the security feed to see how our perimeter was doing. The drones were still patrolling and our sensor alarms all responded to pings.

Overse said, "But why? Why allow a strange group into their habitat? A group whose existence had been concealed from them?"

"You'd do it," I said. I should keep my mouth shut, keep them thinking of me as their normal obedient SecUnit, stop reminding them what I was. But I wanted them to be careful. "If a strange survey group landed here, all friendly, saying they had just arrived, and oh, we've had an equipment failure or our MedSystem's down and we need help, you would let them in. Even if I told you not to, that it was against company safety protocol, you'd do it." Not that I'm bitter, or anything. A lot of the company's rules are stupid or just there to increase profit, but some of them are there for a good reason. Not letting strangers into your habitat is one of them.

Arada and Ratthi exchanged a wry look. Overse conceded, "We might, yes."

Mensah had been quiet, listening to us. She said, "I think it was easier than that. I think they said they were us."

It was so simple, I turned around and looked directly at her. Her brow was furrowed in thought. She said, "So they land, say they're us, that they need help. If they have access to our HubSystem, listening to our comm would be easy."

I said, "When they come here, they won't do that." It all depended on what this other survey group had, whether they had come prepared to get rid of rival survey teams or had decided on it after they got here. They could have armed air vehicles, Combat SecUnits, armed drones. I pulled a few examples from the database and sent them into the feed for the humans to see.

MedSystem's feed informed me that Ratthi, Overse, and Arada's heart rates had just accelerated. Mensah's hadn't, because she had already thought of all this. It was why she had sent Pin-Lee and Gurathin to shut off Hub-System. Nervously, Ratthi said, "What do we do when they come here?"

I said, "Be somewhere else."

It may seem weird that Mensah was the only human to think of abandoning the habitat while we waited for the beacon to bring help, but as I said before, these weren't intrepid galactic explorers. They were people who had been doing a job and suddenly found themselves in a terrible situation.

And it had been hammered into them from the pretrip orientation, to the waivers they had to sign for the company, to the survey packages with all the hazard information, to their on-site briefing by their SecUnit that this was an unknown, potentially dangerous region on a mostly unsurveyed planet. They weren't supposed to leave the habitat without security precautions, and we didn't even do overnight assessment trips. The idea that they might have to stuff both hoppers full of emergency supplies and run for it, and that that would be safer than their habitat, was hard to grasp.

But when Pin-Lee and Gurathin shut down HubSystem, and Volescu unpacked the satellite download that was meant for me, they grasped it pretty quick.

Bharadwaj outlined it for us on the comm while I was getting my last extra suit skin and my armor back on. "It was meant to take control of SecUnit, and the instructions were very specific," she finished. "Once SecUnit was under control, it would give them access to MedSystem and SecSystem."

I got my helmet on and opaqued it. The relief was intense, about even with finding out that the combat override module had been removed. *I love you, armor, and I'm never leaving you again.*

Mensah clicked onto the comm. "Pin-Lee, what about the beacon?"

"I got a go signal when I initiated launch." Pin-Lee sounded even more exasperated than usual. "But with HubSystem shut down, I can't get any confirmation."

I told them over the feed that I could dispatch a drone to check on it. A good beacon launch was pretty important right now. Mensah gave me the go-ahead and I forwarded the order to one of my drones.

Our beacon was a few kilos away from our habitat site for safety, but I thought we should have been able to hear it launch. Maybe not; I had never had to launch one before.

Mensah had already got the humans organized and moving, and as soon as I had my weapons and spare drones loaded, I grabbed a couple of crates. I kept catching little fragments of conversation over the security cameras.

("You have to think of it as a person," Pin-Lee said to Gurathin.

"It *is* a person," Arada insisted.)

Ratthi and Arada sprinted past me carrying medical supplies and spare power cells. I had extended our drone perimeter as far as it could go. We didn't know that whoever hit DeltFall would show up at any second, but it was a strong possibility. Gurathin had come out to check the big hopper and the little hopper's systems, to make sure no one other than us had access and that HubSystem hadn't messed with their code. I kept an eye on him through one of the drones. He kept looking at me, or trying not to look at me, which was worse. I didn't need the distraction right now. When the next attack came, it was going to be fast.

("I do think of it as a person," Gurathin said. "An angry, heavily armed person who has no reason to trust us."

"Then stop being mean to it," Ratthi told him. "That might help.")

"They know their SecUnits successfully gave our SecUnit the combat module," Mensah was saying over the comm. "And we have to assume they received enough information from HubSystem to know we removed it. But they don't know that we've theorized their existence. When SecUnit cut off HubSystem's access, we were still assuming this was sabotage from the company. They won't realize we know they're coming."

Which is why we had to keep moving. Ratthi and

Arada stopped to answer a question about the medical equipment power cells and I shooed them back to the habitat for the next load.

The problem I was going to have is that the way murderbots fight is we throw ourselves at the target and try to kill the shit out of it, knowing that 90 percent of our bodies can be regrown or replaced in a cubicle. So, finesse is not required.

When we left the habitat, I wouldn't have access to the cubicle. Even if we knew how to take it apart, which we didn't, it was too big to fit in the hopper and required too much power.

And they might have actual combat bots rather than security bots like me. In which case, our only chance was going to be keeping away from them until the pick-up transport arrived. If the other survey group hadn't bribed somebody in the company to delay it. I hadn't mentioned that possibility yet.

We had everything almost loaded when Pin-Lee said on the comm, "I found it! They had an access code buried in HubSystem. It wasn't sending them our audio or visual data, or allowing them to see our feed, but it was receiving commands periodically. That's how it removed information from our info and map package, how it sent the command to the little hopper's autopilot to fail."

Gurathin added, "Both the hoppers are clear now and

I've initiated the pre-flight checks."

Mensah was saying something but I had just gotten an alert from SecSystem. A drone was sending me an emergency signal.

A second later I got the drone's visual of the field where our beacon was installed. The tripod launching column was on its side, pieces of the capsule scattered around.

I pushed it out into the general feed, and the humans went quiet. In a little voice, Ratthi said, "Shit."

"Keep moving," Mensah said over the comm, her voice harsh.

With HubSystem down, we didn't have any scanners up, but I had widened the perimeter as far as it would go. And SecSystem had just lost contact with one of the drones to the far south. I tossed the last crate into the cargo hold, gave the drones their orders, and yelled over the comm, "They're coming! We need to get in the air, now!"

It was unexpectedly stressful, pacing back and forth in front of the hoppers waiting for my humans. Volescu came out with Bharadwaj, helping her over the sandy ground. Then Overse and Arada, bags slung over their shoulders, yelling at Ratthi behind them to keep up. Gurathin was already in the big hopper and Mensah and Pin-Lee came last.

They split up, Pin-Lee, Volescu, and Bharadwaj headed for the little hopper and the rest to the big one. I made sure Bharadwaj didn't have trouble with the ramp. We had a problem at the hatch of the big hopper where Mensah wanted to get in last and I wanted to get in last. As a compromise, I grabbed her around the waist and swung us both up into the hatch as the ramp pulled in after us. I set her on her feet and she said, "Thank you, SecUnit," while the others stared.

The helmet made it a little easier, but I was going to miss the comfortable buffer of the security cameras.

I stayed on my feet, holding on to the overhead rail, as the others got strapped in and Mensah went up to the pilot's seat. The little hopper took off first, and she gave it time to get clear before we lifted off.

We were operating on an assumption: that since They, whoever They were, didn't know that we knew They were here, They would only send one ship. They would be expecting to catch us in the habitat, and would probably come in prepared to destroy the hoppers to keep us there, and then start on the people. So now that we knew They were coming from the south, we were free to pick a direction. The little hopper curved away to the west, and we followed.

I just hoped their hopper didn't have a longer range on its scanners than ours did.

I could see most of my drones on the hopper's feed, a bright dot forming on the three dimensions of the map. Group One was doing what I'd told them, gathering at a rendezvous point near the habitat. I had a calculation going, estimating the bogie's time of arrival. Right before we passed out of range I told the drones to head north-east. Within moments, they dropped out of my range. They would follow their last instruction until they used up their power cells.

I was hoping the other survey team would pick them up and follow. As soon as they had a visual on our habitat they'd see the hoppers were gone and know we'd run away. They might stop to search the habitat, but they also might start looking for our escape route. It was impossible to guess which.

But as we flew, curving away to the distant mountains, nothing followed us.

Chapter Six

THE HUMANS HAD DEBATED where to go. Or debated it as much as possible, while frantically calculating how much of what they might need to survive they could stuff into the hoppers. We knew the group who Ratthi was now calling EvilSurvey had had access to HubSystem and knew all the places we'd been to on assessments. So we had to go somewhere new.

We went to a spot Overse and Ratthi had proposed after a quick look at the map. It was a series of rocky hills in a thick tropical jungle, heavily occupied by a large range of fauna, enough to confuse life-sign scans. Mensah and Pin-Lee lowered the hoppers down and eased them in among rocky cliffs. I sent up some drones so we could check the view from several angles and we adjusted the hoppers' positions a few times. Then I set a perimeter.

It didn't feel safe, and while there were a couple of survival hut kits in the hoppers, no one suggested putting them up. The humans would stay in the hoppers for now, communicating over the comm and the hoppers' limited feed. It wasn't going to be comfortable for the humans (sanitary and hygiene facilities were small and limited, for one thing) but it would be more secure. Large and small fauna moved within range of our scanners, curious and potentially as dangerous as the people who wanted to kill my clients.

I went out with some drones to do a little scouting and make sure there was no sign of anything big enough to, say, drag the little hopper off in the middle of the night. It gave me a chance to think, too.

They knew about the governor module, or the lack of it, and even though Mensah had sworn she wouldn't report me, I had to think about what I wanted to do.

It's wrong to think of a construct as half bot, half human. It makes it sound like the halves are discrete, like the bot half should want to obey orders and do its job and the human half should want to protect itself and get the hell out of here. As opposed to the reality, which was that I was one whole confused entity, with no idea what I wanted to do. What I should do. What I needed to do.

I could leave them to cope on their own, I guess. I pictured doing that, pictured Arada or Ratthi trapped by rogue SecUnits, and felt my insides twist. I hate having emotions about reality; I'd much rather have them about *Sanctuary Moon*.

And what was I supposed to do? Go off on this empty planet and just live until my power cells died? If I was going to do that I should have planned better and downloaded more entertainment media. I don't think I could store enough to last until my power cells wore out. My specs told me that would be hundreds of thousands of hours from now.

And even to me, that sounded like a stupid thing to do.

———————

Overse had set up some remote sensing equipment that would help warn us if anything tried to scan the area. As the humans climbed back into the two hoppers, I did a quick headcount on the feed, making sure they were all still there. Mensah waited on the ramp, indicating she wanted to talk to me in private.

I muted my feed and the comm, and she said, "I know you're more comfortable with keeping your helmet opaque, but the situation has changed. We need to see you."

I didn't want to do it. Now more than ever. They knew too much about me. But I needed them to trust me so I could keep them alive and keep doing my job. The good version of my job, not the half-assed version of my job that I'd been doing before things started trying to kill my clients. I still didn't want to do it. "It's usually better if humans think of me as a robot," I said.

"Maybe, under normal circumstances." She was looking a little off to one side, not trying to make eye contact, which I appreciated. "But this situation is different. It would be better if they could think of you as a person who is trying to help. Because that's how I think of you."

My insides melted. That's the only way I could describe it. After a minute, when I had my expression under control, I cleared the face plate and had it and the helmet fold back into my armor.

She said, "Thank you," and I followed her up into the hopper.

The others were stowing the equipment and supplies that had gotten tossed in right before takeoff. "—If they restore the satellite function," Ratthi was saying.

"They won't chance that until—unless they get us," Arada said.

Over the comm, Pin-Lee sighed, angry and frustrated. "If only we knew who these assholes were."

"We need to talk about our next move." Mensah cut through all the chatter and took a seat in the back where she could see the whole compartment. The others sat down to face her, Ratthi turning one of the mobile seats around. I sat down on the bench against the starboard wall. The feed gave us a view of the little hopper's compartment, with the rest of the team sitting there, checking in to show they were listening. Mensah continued,

"There's another question I'd like the answer to."

Gurathin looked at me expectantly. She isn't talking about me, idiot.

Ratthi nodded glumly. "Why? Why are these people doing this? What is worth this to them?"

"It has to have something to do with those blanked-out sections on the map," Overse said. She was calling up the stored images on her feed. "There's obviously something there they want, that they didn't want us or DeltFall to find."

Mensah got up to pace. "Did you turn up anything in the analysis?"

In the feed, Arada did a quick consult with Bharadwaj and Volescu. "Not yet, but we hadn't finished running all the tests. We hadn't turned up anything interesting so far."

"Do they really expect to get away with this?" Ratthi turned to me, like he was expecting an answer. "Obviously, they can hack the company systems and the satellite, and they intend to put the blame on the SecUnits, but . . . The investigation will surely be thorough. They must know this."

There were too many factors in play, and too many things we didn't know, but I'm supposed to answer direct questions and even without the governor module, old habits die hard. "They may believe the company and whoever your beneficiaries are won't look any further than the rogue SecUnits. But they can't make two whole survey teams disappear unless their corporate or political entity doesn't care about them. Does DeltFall's care? Does yours?"

That made them all stare at me, for some reason. I had to turn and look out the port. I wanted to seal my helmet so badly my organic parts started to sweat, but I replayed the conversation with Mensah and managed not to.

Volescu said, "You don't know who we are? They didn't tell you?"

"There was an info packet in my initial download." I was still staring out at the heavy green tangle just past the rocks. I really didn't want to get into how little I paid attention to my job. "I didn't read it."

Arada said, gently, "Why not?"

With all of them staring at me, I couldn't come up with a good lie. "I didn't care."

Gurathin said, "You expect us to believe that."

I felt my face move, my jaw harden. Physical reactions I couldn't suppress. "I'll try to be more accurate. I was indifferent, and vaguely annoyed. Do you believe that?"

He said, "Why don't you want us to look at you?"

My jaw was so tight it triggered a performance reliability alert in my feed. I said, "You don't need to look at me. I'm not a sexbot."

Ratthi made a noise, half sigh, half snort of exaspera-
tion. It wasn't directed at me. He said, "Gurathin, I told
you. It's shy."

Overse added, "It doesn't want to interact with humans. And why should it? You know how constructs are
treated, especially in corporate-political environments."

Gurathin turned to me. "So you don't have a governor
module, but we could punish you by looking at you."

I looked at him. "Probably, right up until I remember I
have guns built into my arms."

With an ironic edge to her voice, Mensah said, "There,
Gurathin. It's threatened you, but it didn't resort to violence. Are you satisfied now?"

He sat back. "For now." So he had been testing me.
Wow, that was brave. And very, very stupid. To me, he
said, "I want to make certain you're not under any outside compulsion."

"That's enough." Arada got up and sat down next to
me. I didn't want to push past her so this pinned me in
the corner. She said, "You need to give it time. It's never
interacted with humans as an openly free agent before
now. This is a learning experience for all of us."

The others nodded, like this made sense.

Mensah sent me a private message through the feed: *I
hope you're all right.*

Because you need me. I don't know where that came

from. All right, it came from me, but she was my client, I was a SecUnit. There was no emotional contract between us. There was no rational reason for me to sound like a whiny human baby.

Of course I need you. I have no experience in anything like this. None of us do. Sometimes humans can't help but let emotion bleed through into the feed. She was furious and frightened, not at me, at the people who would do this, kill like this, slaughter a whole survey team and leave the SecUnits to take the blame. She was struggling with her anger, though nothing showed on her face except calm concern. Through the feed I felt her steel herself. *You're the only one here who won't panic. The longer this situation goes on, the others . . . We have to stay together, use our heads.*

That was absolutely true. And I could help, just by being the SecUnit. I was the one who was supposed to keep everybody safe. *I panic all the time, you just can't see it,* I told her. I added the text signifier for "joke."

She didn't answer, but she looked down, smiling to herself.

Ratthi was saying, "There's another question. Where are they? They came toward our habitat out of the south, but that doesn't tell us anything."

I said, "I left three drones at our habitat. They don't have scanning function with HubSystem down, but the visual and audio recording will still work. They may pick up something that will answer your questions."

I'd left one drone in a tree with a long-range view of the habitat, one tucked under the extendable roof over the entrance, and one inside the hub, hidden under a console. They were on the next setting to inert, recording only, so when EvilSurvey scanned, the drones would be buried in the ambient energy readings from the habitat's environmental system. I hadn't been able to connect the drones to SecSystem like I normally did so it could store the data and filter out the boring parts. I knew EvilSurvey would check for that, which was why I had dumped Sec-System's storage into the big hopper's system and then purged it.

I also didn't want them knowing any more about me than they already did.

Everyone was looking at me again, surprised that Murderbot had had a plan. Frankly, I didn't blame them. Our education modules didn't have anything like that in it, but this was another way all the thrillers and adventures I'd watched or read were finally starting to come in handy. Mensah lifted her brows in appreciation. She said, "But you can't pick up their signal from here."

"No, I'll have to go back to get the data," I told her.

Pin-Lee leaned farther into the little hopper's camera range. "I should be able to attach one of the small scanners to a drone. It'll be bulky and slow, but that would give us something other than just audio and visual."

Mensah nodded. "Do it, but remember our resources are limited." She tapped me in the feed so I'd know she was talking to me without her looking at me. "How long do you think the other group will stay at our habitat?"

There was a groan from Volescu in the other hopper. "All our samples. We have our data, but if they destroy our work—"

The others were agreeing with him, expressing frustration and worry. I tuned them out, and answered Mensah, "I don't think they'll stay long. There's nothing there they want."

For just an instant, Mensah let her expression show how worried she was. "Because they want us," she said softly.

She was absolutely right about that, too.

———————

Mensah set up a watch schedule, including in time for me to go into standby and do a diagnostic and recharge cycle. I was also planning to use the time to watch some *Sanctuary Moon* and recharge my ability to cope with humans at close quarters without losing my mind.

After the humans had settled down, either sleeping

or deep in their own feeds, I walked the perimeter and checked the drones. The night was noisier than the day, but so far nothing bigger than insects and a few reptiles had come near the hoppers. When I cycled through the big hopper's hatch, Ratthi was the human on watch, sitting up in the cockpit and keeping an eye on its scanners. I moved up past the crew section and sat next to him. He nodded to me and said, "All's well?"

"Yes." I didn't want to, but I had to ask. When I was looking for permanent storage for all my entertainment downloads, the info packet was one of the files I'd purged. (I know, but I'm used to having all the extra storage on SecSystem.) Remembering what Mensah had said, I unsealed my helmet. It was easier with just Ratthi, both of us facing toward the console. "Why did everyone think it was so strange that I asked if your political entity would miss you?"

Ratthi smiled at the console. "Because Dr. Mensah is our political entity." He made a little gesture, turning his hand palm up. "We're from Preservation Alliance, one of the non-corporate system entities. Dr. Mensah is the current admin director on the steering committee. It's an elected position, with a limited term. But one of the principles of our home is that our admins must also continue their regular work, whatever it is. Her regular work required this survey, so here she is, and here we are."

Yeah, I felt a little stupid. I was still processing it when he said, "You know, in Preservation-controlled territory, bots are considered full citizens. A construct would fall under the same category." He said this in the tone of giving me a hint.

Whatever. Bots who are "full citizens" still have to have a human or augmented human guardian appointed, usually their employer; I'd seen it on the news feeds. And the entertainment feed, where the bots were all happy servants or were secretly in love with their guardians. If it showed the bots hanging out watching the entertainment feed all through the day cycle with no one trying to make them talk about their feelings, I would have been a lot more interested. "But the company knows who she is."

Ratthi sighed. "Oh, yes, they know. You would not believe what we had to pay to guarantee the bond on the survey. These corporate arseholes are robbers."

It meant if we ever managed to launch the beacon, the company wouldn't screw around, the transport would get here fast. No bribe from EvilSurvey could stop it. They might even send a faster security ship to check out the problem before the transport could arrive. The bond on a political leader was high, but the payout the company would have to make if something happened to her was off the chart. The huge payout, being humiliated in front of the other bond companies and in the news feeds . . . I leaned back in my seat and sealed my helmet to think about it.

We didn't know who EvilSurvey was, who we were dealing with. But I bet that they didn't either. Mensah's status was only in the Security info packet, stored on Sec-System, which they had never gotten access to. The dueling investigations if something happened to us were bound to be thorough, as the company would be desperate for something to blame it on and the beneficiaries would be desperate to blame it on the company. Neither would be fooled long by the rogue SecUnit setup.

I didn't see how we could use it, not right now, anyway. It didn't comfort me and I'm pretty sure it wouldn't comfort the humans to know the stupid company would avenge them if/when they all got murdered.

———————

So midafternoon the next day I got ready to take the little hopper back within range of the habitat so I could hopefully pick up intel from the drones. I wanted to go alone, but since nobody ever listens to me, Mensah, Pin-Lee, and Ratthi were going, too.

I was depressed this morning. I'd tried watching some new serials last night and even they couldn't distract me;

reality was too intrusive. It was hard not to think about how everything was going to go wrong and they were all going to die and I was going to get blasted to pieces or get another governor module stuck in me.

Gurathin walked up to me while I was doing the pre-flight, and said, "I'm coming with you."

That was about all I needed right now. I finished the diagnostic on the power cells. "I thought you were satisfied."

It took him a minute. "What I said last night, yes."

"I remember every word ever said to me." That was a lie. Who would want that? Most of it I delete from permanent memory.

He didn't say anything. On the feed, Mensah told me that I didn't have to take him if I didn't want to, or if I thought it would compromise team security. I knew Gurathin was testing me again, but if something went wrong and he got killed, I wouldn't mind as much as I would if it was one of the others. I wished Mensah, Ratthi, and Pin-Lee weren't coming; I didn't want to risk them. And on the long trip, Ratthi might be tempted to try to make me talk about my feelings.

I told Mensah it was fine, and we got ready to lift off.

———

I wanted a long time to circle west, so if EvilSurvey picked us up they wouldn't be able to extrapolate the humans' location from my course. By the time I was in position for the approach to the habitat, the light was failing. When we got to the target zone, it would be full dark.

The humans hadn't gotten a lot of sleep last night, from the crowding and the strong possibility of dying. Mensah, Ratthi, and Pin-Lee had been too tired to talk much, and had fallen asleep. Gurathin was sitting in the copilot's seat and hadn't said a word the whole time.

We were flying in dark mode, with no lights, no transmissions. I was plugged in to the little hopper's internal limited feed so I could watch the scans carefully. Gurathin was aware of the feed through his implant—I could feel him in there—but wasn't using it except to keep track of where we were.

When he said, "I have a question," I flinched. The silence up to this point had lulled me into a false sense of security.

I didn't look at him though I knew through the feed that he was looking at me. I hadn't closed my helmet; I didn't feel like hiding from him. After a moment I realized he was waiting for my permission. That was weirdly new. It was tempting to ignore him, but I was wondering what the test would be this time. Something he didn't want the others to hear? I said, "Go ahead."

He said, "Did they punish you, for the deaths of the mining team?"

It wasn't completely a surprise. I think they all wanted to ask about it, but maybe he was the only one abrasive enough. Or brave enough. It's one thing to poke a murderbot with a governor module; poking a rogue murderbot is a whole different proposition.

I said, "No, not like you're thinking. Not the way a human would be punished. They shut me down for a while, and then brought me back online at intervals."

He hesitated. "You weren't aware of it?"

Yeah, that would be the easy way out, wouldn't it? "The organic parts mostly sleep, but not always. You know something's happening. They were trying to purge my memory. We're too expensive to destroy."

He looked out the port again. We were flying low over trees, and I had a lot of my attention on the terrain sensors. I felt the brush of Mensah's awareness in the feed. She must have woken when Gurathin spoke. He finally said, "You don't blame humans for what you were forced to do? For what happened to you?"

This is why I'm glad I'm not human. They come up with stuff like this. I said, "No. That's a human thing to do. Constructs aren't that stupid."

What was I supposed to do, kill all humans because the ones in charge of constructs in the company were cal-

lous? Granted, I liked the imaginary people on the entertainment feed way more than I liked real ones, but you
can't have one without the other.

The others started to stir, waking and sitting up, and he
didn't ask me anything else.

By the time we got within range, it was a cloudless night
with the ring glowing in the sky like a ribbon. I had already dropped speed, and we were moving slowly over
the sparse trees decorating the hills at the edge of the
habitat's plain. I had been waiting for the drones to ping
me, which they would if this had worked and EvilSurvey
hadn't found them.

When I felt that first cautious touch on my feed, I
stopped the hopper and dropped it down below the tree
line. I landed on a hillside, the hopper's pads extending to
compensate. The humans were waiting, nervy and impatient, but no one spoke. You couldn't see anything from
here except the next hill and a lot of tree trunks.

All three drones were still active. I answered the pings,
trying to keep my transmission as quick as possible. After
a tense moment, the downloads started. I could tell from
the timestamps that, with nobody there to instruct them
not to, the drones had recorded everything from the mo-

ment I'd deployed them to now. Even though the part we were most interested in would be near the beginning, that was a lot of data. I didn't want to stay here long enough to parse it myself, so I pushed half of it into the feed for Gurathin. Again, he didn't say anything, just turned in his chair to lie back, close his eyes, and start reviewing it.

I checked the drone stationed outside in the tree first, running its video at high speed until I found the moment where it had caught a good image of the Evil-Survey craft.

It was a big hopper, a newer model than ours, nothing about it to cause anybody any pause. It circled the habitat a few times, probably scanning, and then landed on our empty pad.

They must know we were gone, with no air craft on the pad and no answer on their comm, so they didn't bother to pretend to be here to borrow some tools or exchange site data. Five SecUnits piled out of the cargo pods, all armed with the big projectile weapons assigned to protect survey teams on planets with hazardous fauna, like this one. From the pattern on the armor chestplates, two were the surviving DeltFall units. They must have been put into their cubicles after we escaped the DeltFall habitat.

Three were EvilSurvey, which had a square gray logo. I

focused in on it and sent it to the others. "GrayCris," Pin-Lee read aloud.

"Ever heard of it?" Ratthi said, and the others said no.

All five SecUnits would have the combat override modules installed. They started toward the habitat, and five humans, anonymous in their color-coded field suits, climbed out of the hopper and followed. They were all armed, too, with the handweapons the company provided, that were only supposed to be used for fauna-related emergencies.

I focused as far in on the humans as the image quality would allow. They spent a lot of time scanning and checking for traps, which made me even more glad I hadn't wasted time setting any. But there was something about them that made me think I wasn't looking at professionals. They weren't soldiers, any more than I was. Their SecUnits weren't combat units, just regular security rented from the company. That was a relief. At least I wasn't the only one who didn't know what I was doing.

Finally I watched them enter the habitat, leaving two SecUnits outside to guard their hopper. I tagged the section, passed it to Mensah and the others for review, and then kept watching.

Gurathin sat up suddenly and muttered a curse in a language I didn't know. I noted it to look up later on the big hopper's language center. Then forgot about it when he said, "We have a problem."

I put my part of the drones' download on pause and looked at the section he had just tagged. It was from the drone hidden in the hub.

The visual was a blurred image of a curved support strut but the audio was a human voice saying, "You knew we were coming, so I assume you have some way to watch us while we're here." The voice spoke standard lexicon with a flat accent. "We've destroyed your beacon. Come to these coordinates—" She spoke a set of longitude and latitude numbers that the little hopper helpfully mapped for me, and a time stamp. "—at this time, and we can come to some arrangement. This doesn't have to end in violence. We're happy to pay you off, or whatever you want."

There was nothing else, steps fading until the door slid shut.

Gurathin, Pin-Lee, and Ratthi all started to speak at once. Mensah said, "Quiet." They shut up. "SecUnit, your opinion."

Fortunately, I had one now. Up to the point where we'd gotten the drone download, my opinion had been mostly *oh, shit*. I said, "They have nothing to lose. If we come to this rendezvous, they can kill us and stop worrying about us. If we don't, they have until the end of project date to search for us."

Gurathin was reviewing the landing video now. He said, "Another indication it isn't the company. They obviously don't want to chase us until the end of project date."

I said, "I told you it wasn't the company."

Mensah interrupted Gurathin before he could respond. "They think we know why they're here, why they're doing this."

"They're wrong," Ratthi said, frustrated.

Mensah's brow furrowed as she picked apart the problem for the other humans. "But why do they think that? It must be because they know we went to one of the unmapped regions. That means the data we collected must have the answer."

Pin-Lee nodded. "So the others may know by now."

"It gives us leverage," Mensah said thoughtfully. "But what can we do with it?"

And then I had a great idea.

Chapter Seven

SO AT THE APPOINTED time the next day, Mensah and I were flying toward the rendezvous point.

Gurathin and Pin-Lee had taken one of my drones and rebuilt it with a limited scanning attachment. (Limited because the drone was too small for most of the components a longer and wider range scanner would need.) Last night I had sent it into upper atmosphere to give us a view of the site.

The location was near their survey base, which was only about two kilos away, a habitat similar to DeltFall's. By the size of their habitat and the number of SecUnits, including the one Mensah had taken out with a mining drill, they had between thirty and forty team members. They were obviously very confident, but then, they'd had access to our hub and they knew they were dealing with a small group of scientists and researchers, and one messed-up secondhand SecUnit.

I just hoped they didn't realize how messed up I actually was.

When the hopper picked up the first blip of scanner

contact, Mensah hit the comm immediately. "GrayCris, be advised that my party has secured evidence of your activities on this planet, and hidden it in various places where it will transmit to the pickup ship whenever it arrives." She let that sink in for three seconds, then added, "You know we found the missing map sections."

There was a long pause. I was slowing us down, scanning for incoming weapons, even though the chances were good they didn't have any.

The comm channel came alive, and a voice said, "We can discuss our situation. An arrangement can be made." There was so much scanning and anti-scanning going on the voice was made of static. It was creepy. "Land your vehicle and we can discuss it."

Mensah gave it a minute, as if she was thinking it over, then answered, "I'll send our SecUnit to speak to you." She cut the comm off.

As we got closer we had a visual on the site. It was a low plateau, surrounded by trees. Their habitat was visible to the west. Because the trees encroached on their camp site, their domes and vehicle landing pad were elevated on wide platforms. The company required this as a security feature if you wanted your base to be anywhere without open terrain around it. It cost extra, and if you didn't want it, it cost even more to guarantee your bond. It was one of the reasons I thought my great idea would work.

In the open area on the plateau were seven figures, four SecUnits and three humans in the color-coded enviro suits, blue, green, and yellow. It meant they had one SecUnit and probably twenty seven–plus humans back at their habitat, if they had followed the rule of one rental SecUnit per ten humans. I sat us down below the plateau, on a relatively flat rock, the view blocked by brush and trees.

I put the pilot's console on standby, and looked at Mensah. She pressed her lips together, like she wanted to say something and was repressing the urge. Then she nodded firmly and said, "Good luck."

I felt like I should say something to her, and didn't know what, and just stared at her awkwardly for a few seconds. Then I sealed up my helmet and got out of the hopper as fast as I could.

I went through the trees, listening for that fifth SecUnit just in case it was hiding somewhere waiting for me, but there was no sound of movement in the undergrowth. I came out of cover and climbed the rocky slope to the plateau, then walked toward the other group, listening to the crackle on my comm. They were going to let me get close, which was a relief. I'd hate to be wrong about this. It would make me feel pretty stupid.

I stopped several meters away, opened the channel and said, "This is the SecUnit assigned to the PreservationAux Survey Team. I was sent to speak to you about an arrangement."

I felt the pulse then, a signal bundle, designed to take over my governor module and freeze it, and freeze me. The idea was obviously to immobilize me, then insert the combat override module into my dataport again.

That was why they had had to arrange the meeting so close to their hub. They had needed the equipment there to be able to do this, it wasn't something they could send through the feed.

So it's a good thing my governor module wasn't working and all I felt was a mild tickle.

One of them started toward me. I said, "I assume you're about to try to install another combat override module and send me back to kill them." I opened my gun ports and expanded the weapons in my arms, then folded them back in. "I don't recommend that course of action."

The SecUnits went into alert mode. The human who had started forward froze, then backed away. The body language of the others was flustered, startled. I could tell from the faint comm static that they were talking to each other on their own system. I said, "Anyone want to comment on that?"

That got their attention. There was no reply. Not a surprise. The only people I've run into who actually want to get into conversations with SecUnits are my weird humans. I said, "I have an alternate solution to both our problems."

The one in the blue enviro suit said, "You have a solution?" The voice was the same one who had made the offer in our hub. It was also very skeptical, which you can imagine. To them, talking to me was like talking to a hopper or a piece of mining equipment.

I said, "You weren't the first to hack PreservationAux's HubSystem."

She had opened their comm channel to talk to me, and I heard one of the others whisper, "It's a trick. One of the surveyors is telling it what to say."

I said, "Your scans should show I've cut my comm." This was the point where I had to say it. It was still hard, even though I knew I didn't have a choice, even though it was part of my own stupid plan. "I don't have a working governor module." That over, I was glad to get back to the lying part. "They don't know that. I'm amenable to a compromise that benefits you as well as me."

The blue leader said, "Are they telling the truth about knowing why we're here?"

That was still annoying, even though I knew we had allowed plenty of time for this part. "You used combat override modules to make the DeltFall SecUnits behave like rogues. If you think a real rogue SecUnit still has to answer your questions, the next few minutes are going to be an education for you."

The blue leader shut me out of their comm channel. There was a long silence while they talked it over. Then she came back on, and said, "What compromise?"

"I can give you information you desperately need. In exchange, you take me onto the pick-up ship with you but list me as destroyed inventory." That would mean nobody from the company would be expecting me back, and I could slip off in the confusion when the transport docked at the transit station. Theoretically.

There was another hesitation. Because they had to pretend to think it over, I guess. Then the blue leader said, "We agree. If you're lying, then we'll destroy you."

It was perfunctory. They intended to insert a combat override module into me before they left the planet.

She continued, "What is the information?"

I said, "First remove me from the inventory. I know you still have a connection to our Hub."

Blue Leader made an impatient gesture at Yellow. He said, "We'll have to restart their HubSystem. That will take some time."

I said, "Initiate the restart, queue the command, and then show me on your feed. Then I'll give you the information."

Blue Leader closed me out of the comm channel and spoke to Yellow again. There was a three-minute wait, then the channel opened again and I got a limited access to their feed. The command was in a queue, though of course they would have time to delete it later. The important points were that our HubSystem had been reactivated, and that I could convincingly pretend to believe them. I had been watching the time, and we were now in the target window, so there was no more reason to stall. I said, "Since you destroyed my clients' beacon, they've sent a group to your beacon to manually trigger it."

Even with limited access to their feed, I could see that got them. Body language all over the place from confusion to fear. The yellow one moved uncertainly, the green one looked at Blue Leader. In that flat accent, she said, "That's impossible."

I said, "One of them is an augmented human, a systems engineer. He can make it launch. Check the data you got from our HubSystem. It's Surveyor Dr. Gurathin."

Blue Leader was showing tension from her shoulders all down her body. She really didn't want anybody coming to this planet, not until they had taken care of their witness problem.

Green said, "It's lying."

A trace of panic in his voice, Yellow said, "We can't chance it."

Blue Leader turned to him. "It's possible, then?"

Yellow hesitated. "I don't know. The company systems are all proprietary, but if they have an augmented human who can hack into it—"

"We have to go there now," Blue Leader said. She turned to me. "SecUnit, tell your client to get out of the hopper and come here. Tell her we've come to an arrangement."

All right, wow. That was not in the plan. They were supposed to leave without us.

(Last night Gurathin had said this was a weak point, that this was where the plan would fall apart. It was irritating that he was right.)

I couldn't open my comm channel to the hopper or the hopper's feed without GrayCris knowing. And we still needed to get them and their SecUnits away from their habitat. I said, "She knows you mean to kill her. She won't come." Then I had another brilliant idea and added, "She's a planetary admin for a system noncorporate political entity, she's not stupid."

"What?" Green demanded. "What political entity?"

I said, "Why do you think the team is called 'Preservation'?"

This time they didn't bother to close their channel. Yellow said, "We can't kill her. The investigation—"

Green added, "He's right. We can hold her and release her after the settlement agreement."

Blue Leader snapped, "That won't work. If she's missing, the investigation would be even more thorough. We need to stop that beacon launch, then we can discuss what to do." She told me, "Go get her. Get her out of the hopper and then bring her here." She cut the comm off again. Then one of the DeltFall SecUnits started forward. She came back on to say, "This Unit will help you."

I waited for it to reach me, then turned and walked beside it down the slope of rock into the trees.

What I did next was predicated on the assumption that she had told the DeltFall SecUnit to kill me. If I was wrong, we were screwed, and Mensah and I would both die, and the plan to save the rest of the group would fail and PreservationAux would be back to where it started, except minus their leader, their SecUnit, and their little hopper.

As we left the rocky slope and turned into the trees, the brush and branches screening us from the edge of the plateau, I slung an arm around the other Unit's neck, deployed my arm weapon, and fired into the side of its helmet where its comm channel was. It went down on one knee, swinging its projectile weapon toward me, energy weapons unfolding out of its armor.

With the combat override module in place, its feed was cut off, and with its comm down it couldn't yell for help. Also, depending on how strictly they had limited its voluntary actions, it might not be able to call for help unless the GrayCris humans told it to. Maybe that was the case, because all it did was try to kill me. We rolled over rock and brush until I wrenched its weapon away. After that it was easy to finish it off. Physically easy.

I know I said SecUnits aren't sentimental about each other, but I wished it wasn't one of the DeltFall units. It was in there somewhere, trapped in its own head, maybe aware, maybe not. Not that it matters. None of us had a choice.

I stood up just as Mensah slammed through the brush, carrying the mining tool. I told her, "It's gone wrong. You have to pretend to be my prisoner."

She looked at me, then looked at the DeltFall unit. "How are you going to explain that?"

I started shedding armor, every piece that had a PreservationAux logo on it, and leaned over the DeltFall unit as the pieces dropped away. "I'm going to be it and it's going to be me."

Mensah dropped the mining tool and bent down to help me. We didn't have time to switch all the armor. Moving fast, we replaced the arm and shoulder pieces on both sides, the leg pieces that had the armor's inventory code, the chest and back piece with the logos. Mensah smeared my remaining armor pieces with dirt and blood and fluid from the dead unit, so if we had missed anything distinctive GrayCris might not notice. SecUnits are identical in height and build, the way we moved. This might work. I don't know. If we ran away now the plan would fail, we had to get them off this plateau. As I re-sealed the helmet, I told Mensah, "We have to go—"

She nodded, breathing hard, more from nerves than exertion. "I'm ready."

I took her arm, and pretended to drag her back toward the GrayCris group. She yelled and struggled convincingly the whole way.

When we reached the plateau, a GrayCris hopper was already landing.

As I pulled her toward Blue Leader, Mensah got in the first word. She said, "So this is the arrangement you of-fered?"

Blue Leader said, "You're the planetary admin of Preservation?"

Mensah didn't look at me. If they tried to hurt her, I'd try to stop them and everything would go horribly wrong. But Green was already getting into the hopper. Two other humans were in the pilot's and copilot's seats. Mensah said, "Yes."

Yellow came toward me and touched the side of my helmet. It took a tremendous effort for me not to rip his arm off, and I'd like that noted for the record, please. He said, "Its comm is down."

To Mensah, Blue Leader said, "We know one of your people is trying to manually trigger our beacon. If you come with us, we won't harm him, and we can discuss our situation. This doesn't have to go badly for either of us." She was very convincing. She had probably been the one to talk to DeltFall on the comm, asking to be let into their habitat.

Mensah hesitated, and I knew she didn't want it to look like she was giving in too quickly, but we had to get them out of there now. She said, "Very well."

I hadn't ridden in the cargo container for a while. It would have been comforting and homey, except it wasn't my cargo container.

But this hopper was still a company product and I was able to access its feed. I had to stay very quiet, to keep them from noticing me, but all those hours of surreptitiously consuming media came in handy.

Their SecSystem was still recording. They must mean to delete all that before the pick-up transport showed up. Client groups had tried that before, to hide data from the company so it couldn't be sold out from under them, and the company systems analysts would be on the alert for it, but I don't know if these people realized that. The company might catch them even if we didn't survive. That wasn't a very comforting thought.

As I accessed the ongoing recording, I heard Mensah saying, "—know about the remnants in the unmapped areas. They were strong enough to confuse our mapping functions. Is that how you found them?"

Bharadwaj had figured that out last night. The unmapped sections weren't an intentional hack, they were an error, caused by the remnants that were buried under the dirt and rock. This planet had been inhabited at some point in its past, which meant it would be placed under interdict, open only to archeological surveys. Even the company would abide by that.

You could make big, illegal money off of excavating and mining those remnants, and that was obviously what GrayCris wanted.

"That isn't the conversation we should be having," Blue Leader said. "I want to know what arrangement we can come to."

"To keep you from killing us like you did DeltFall," Mensah said, keeping her voice even. "Once we're in contact with our home again, we can arrange for a transfer of funds. But how can we trust you to leave us alive?"

There was a little silence. Oh great, they don't know either. Then Blue Leader said, "You have no option except to trust us."

We were slowing down already, coming in for a landing. There had been no alerts on the feed and I was cautiously optimistic. We had cleared the field for Pin-Lee and Gurathin as much as we could. They had had to hack the perimeter without that one last SecUnit noticing and get close enough to access the GrayCris HubSystem feed. (Hopefully it was the last SecUnit, hopefully there weren't a dozen more somehow in the GrayCris habitat.) Gurathin had figured out how to use the hack from their HubSystem into our HubSystem to get access, but he needed to be close to their habitat to actually trigger their beacon. That was why we had to get the other SecUnits out of there. That was the idea, anyway. Possibly it would have worked without putting Mensah in danger but it was a little late to second-guess everything.

It was a relief when we thumped down into a landing that must have made the humans' teeth rattle. I deployed out of the pod with the other units.

We were a few kilos from their habitat, on a big rock above a thick forest, lots of avians and other fauna screaming down in the trees, disturbed by the hopper's hard landing. Clouds had come in, threatening rain, and obscuring the view of the ring. The beacon's vehicle was in a launch tripod about ten meters away and, uh-oh, that is way too close.

I joined the three other SecUnits as we made a standard security formation. An array of drones launched from the craft to create a perimeter. I didn't look at the humans as they walked down the ramp. I really wanted to look at Mensah for instructions. If I was alone, I could have sprinted for the end of the plateau, but I had to get her out of there.

Blue Leader stepped forward with Green; the others gathered in a loose circle behind her, like they were afraid to get in front. One, who must have been getting reports from their SecUnits and drones, said, "No sign of anybody." Blue Leader didn't answer but the two GrayCris SecUnits jogged toward the beacon.

Okay, the problem is, I've mentioned this before, the company is cheap. When it comes to something like a beacon that just has to launch once if there's an emergency, send a transmission through the wormhole, and then never gets retrieved, they're very cheap. Beacons don't have safety features, and use the cheapest possible launch vehicles. There's a reason you put them a few kilos from your habitat and trigger them from a distance. Mensah and I were supposed to distract GrayCris and their SecUnits while this was going on, get them away from the habitat, not end up as toast in the beacon launch.

With the delay caused by Blue Leader deciding to grab Mensah, time was getting close. The two SecUnits were circling the beacon's tripod, looking for signs of tampering, and I couldn't take it anymore. I started to walk toward Mensah.

Yellow noticed me. He must have said something to Blue Leader on their feed because she turned to look at me.

When the remaining DeltFall SecUnit whipped toward me and opened fire, I knew the light had dawned. I dove and rolled, coming up with my projectile weapon. I was taking hits all over my armor but scoring hits on the other SecUnit. Mensah ducked around the other side of the hopper and I felt a thump rattle through the plateau. That was the beacon's primary drive, dropping out of its casing to the bottom of the tripod, getting ready to ignite. The other two SecUnits had stopped, Blue Leader's surprise freezing them in place.

I bolted, took a hit in a weak armor joint that went through to my thigh, and powered through it. I made it around the hopper and saw Mensah. I tackled her off the edge of the rock, turning to land on my back, curling an arm over her suit helmet to protect her head from impact. We bounced off rocks and crashed through trees, then fire washed over the plateau and knocked out my—

```
unit offline
```

Oh, that hurt. I was lying in a ravine, rocks and trees

overhanging it. Mensah was sitting next to me, cradling an arm that looked like it didn't work anymore and her suit was covered with tears and stains.

She was whispering to someone on the comm. "Careful, if they pick you up on their scanner—"

```
unit offline
```

"That's why we need to hurry," Gurathin said, who was suddenly standing over us. I realized I had lost some time again.

Gurathin and Pin-Lee had been on foot, making their way toward the GrayCris habitat through the cover of the forest. We had meant to go pick them up in the little hopper if everything didn't go to shit. Which it did, but only partly, so yay for that.

Pin-Lee leaned over me and I said, "This unit is at minimal functionality and it is recommended that you discard it." It's an automatic reaction triggered by catastrophic malfunction. Also, I really didn't want them to try to move me because it hurt bad enough the way it was. "Your contract allows—"

"Shut up," Mensah snapped. "You shut the fuck up. We're not leaving you."

My visual cut out again. I was sort of still there, but I could tell I was hovering on the edge of a systems failure.

I had flashes off and on. The inside of the little hopper, my humans talking, Arada holding my hand.

Then being in the big hopper, as it was lifting up. I could tell from the drive noise, the flashes of the feed, that the pick-up transport was bringing it onboard.

That was a relief. It meant they were all safe, and I let go.

Chapter Eight

I CAME BACK TO awareness in a cubicle, the familiar acrid odor and hum of the systems as it put me back together. Then I realized it wasn't the cubicle at the habitat. It was an older model, a permanent installation.

I was back at the company station.

And humans knew about my governor module.

I poked tentatively at it. Still nonfunctional. My media storage was still intact, too. Huh.

When the cubicle opened, Ratthi was standing there. He was wearing regular civilian station clothes, but with the soft gray jacket with the PreservationAux survey logo. He looked happy, and a lot cleaner than the last time I had seen him. He said, "Good news! Dr. Mensah has permanently bought your contract! You're coming home with us!"

That was a surprise.

———

I went to finish processing, still reeling. It seemed like

the kind of thing that would happen in a show, so I kept running diagnostics and checking the various available feeds to make sure I wasn't still in the cubicle, hallucinating. There was a report running on the local station news about DeltFall and GrayCris and the investigation. If I was hallucinating, I think the company wouldn't have managed to come out of the whole mess as the heroic rescuers of PreservationAux.

I expected a suit skin and armor, but the station units that helped us out of processing when we had catastrophic injuries gave me the gray PreservationAux survey uniform instead. I put it on, feeling weird, while the station units stood around and watched me. We're not buddies or anything, but usually they pass along the news, what happened while you were offline, what the upcoming contracts were. I wondered if they felt as weird as I did. Sometimes SecUnits got bought in groups, complete with cubicles, by other companies. Nobody had ever come back from a survey and decided they wanted to keep their unit.

When I came out Ratthi was still there. He grabbed my arm and tugged me past a couple of human techs and out through two levels of secure doors and into the display area. This was where the rentals were arranged and it was nicer than the rest of the deployment center, with carpets and couches. Pin-Lee stood in the middle of it, dressed in sharp business attire. She looked like somebody from one of the shows I liked. The tough yet compassionate solicitor coming to rescue us from unfair prosecution. Two humans in company gear were standing around like they wanted to argue with her but she was ignoring them, tossing a data chip casually in one hand.

One saw me and Ratthi and said, "Again, this is irregular. Purging the unit's memory before it changes hands isn't just a policy, it's best for the—"

"Again, I have a court order," Pin-Lee said, grabbed my other arm, and they walked me out.

I had never seen the human parts of the station before. We went down the big multilevel center ring, past office blocks and shopping centers, crowded with every kind of people, every kind of bot, flash data displays darting around, a hundred different public feeds brushing my awareness. It was just like a place from the entertainment feed but bigger and brighter and noisier. It smelled good, too.

The thing that surprised me is that nobody stared at us. Nobody even gave us a second look. The uniform, the pants, the long-sleeved T-shirt and jacket, covered all my inorganic parts. If they noticed the dataport in the back of my neck they must have thought I was an augmented human. We were just three more people making our way down the ring. It hit me that I was just as anonymous in a crowd of humans who didn't know each other as I was in my armor, in a group of other SecUnits.

As we turned into a hotel block I brushed a public feed offering station info. I saved a map and a set of shift schedules as we passed through the doors into the lobby.

There were potted trees twisting up into a hanging glass sculpture fountain, real, not a holo. Looking at it I almost didn't see the reporters until they were right up on us. They were augmented humans, with a couple of drone cams. One tried to stop Pin-Lee, and instinct took over and I shouldered him off her.

He looked startled but I'd been gentle so he didn't fall down. Pin-Lee said, "We're not taking questions now," shoved Ratthi into the hotel's transport pod, then grabbed my arm and pulled me in after her.

It whooshed us around and let us out in the foyer of a big suite. I followed Pin-Lee in, Ratthi behind us talking to someone on his comm. It was just as fancy as the ones on the media, with carpets and furniture and big windows looking down on the garden and sculptures in the main lobby. Except the rooms were smaller. I guess the ones in the shows are bigger, to give them better angles for the drone cams.

My clients—ex-clients? New owners?—were here, only everybody looked different in their normal clothes.

Dr. Mensah stepped close, looking up at me. "Are you all right?"

"Yes." I had clear pictures from my field camera of her being hurt, but all her damage had been repaired, too. She looked different, in business clothes like Pin-Lee's. "I don't understand what's happening." It was stressful. I could feel the entertainment feed out there, the same one I could access from the unit processing zone, and it was hard not to sink into it.

She said, "I've purchased your contract. You're coming back to Preservation with us. You'll be a free agent there."

"I'm off inventory." They had told me that and maybe it was true. I had the urge to twitch uncontrollably and I had no idea why. "Can I still have armor?" It was the armor that told people I was a SecUnit. But I wasn't Sec anymore, just Unit.

The others were so quiet. She said, even and calm, "We can arrange that, as long as you think you need it."

I didn't know if I thought I needed it or not. "I don't have a cubicle."

She was reassuring. "You won't need one. People won't be shooting at you. If you're hurt, or your parts are damaged, you can be repaired in a medical center."

"If people won't be shooting at me what will I be doing?" Maybe I could be her bodyguard.

"I think you can learn to do anything you want." She smiled. "We'll talk about that when we get you home."

Arada walked in then, and came over and patted my shoulder. "We're so glad you're with us," she said. She told Mensah, "The DeltFall representatives are here."

Mensah nodded. "I have to talk to them," she told me. "Make yourself comfortable here. If there's anything you need, tell us."

I sat in a back corner and watched while different people came in and out of the suite to talk about what had happened. Solicitors, mostly. From the company, from DeltFall, from at least three other corporate political entities and one independent, even from GrayCris' parent company. They asked questions, argued, looked at security records, showed Mensah and Pin-Lee security records. And they looked at me. Gurathin watched me, too, but he didn't say anything. I wondered if he had told Mensah not to buy me.

I watched the entertainment feed a little to calm down, then pulled everything I could about the Preservation Alliance from the station's information center. No one would be shooting at me because they didn't shoot people there. Mensah didn't need a bodyguard there; nobody did. It sounded like a great place to live, if you were a human or augmented human.

Ratthi came over to see if I was all right, and I asked him to tell me about Preservation and how Mensah lived there. He said when she wasn't doing admin work, she lived on a farm outside the capital city, with two marital partners, plus her sister and brother and their three marital partners, and a bunch of relatives and kids who Ratthi had lost count of. He was called away to answer questions from a solicitor, which gave me time to think.

I didn't know what I would do on a farm. Clean the house? That sounded way more boring than security. Maybe it would work out. This was what I was supposed to want. This was what everything had always told me I was supposed to want.

Supposed to want.

I'd have to pretend to be an augmented human, and that would be a strain. I'd have to change, make myself do things I didn't want to do. Like talk to humans like I was one of them. I'd have to leave the armor behind.

But maybe I wouldn't need it anymore.

———

Eventually things settled down, and they had dinner brought in. Mensah came and talked to me some more, about Preservation, what my options would be there, how I would stay with her until I knew what I wanted.

It was pretty much what I'd already figured, from what Ratthi had told me.

"You'd be my guardian," I said.

"Yes." She was glad I understood. "There are so many education opportunities. You can do anything you want."

Guardian was a nicer word than owner.

I waited until the middle of the offshift, when they were all either asleep or deep in their own feeds, working on their analysis of the assessment materials. I got up from the couch and went down the corridor, and slipped out the door.

I used the transport pod and got back to the lobby, then left the hotel. I had the map I had downloaded earlier, so I knew how to get off the ring and down toward the lower port work zones. I was wearing a survey team uniform, and passing as an augmented human, so nobody stopped me, or looked twice at me.

At the edge of the work zone, I went through into the dockworkers' barracks, then into the equipment storage. Besides tools, the human workers had storage cubbies there. I broke into a human's personal possessions locker and stole work boots, a protective jacket, and an enviro mask and attachments. I took a knapsack from another locker, rolled up the jacket with the survey logo and tucked it into the bag, and now I looked like an augmented human traveling somewhere. I walked out of the work zones and down the big central corridor into the port's embarkation zone, just one of hundreds of travelers heading for the ship ring.

I checked the schedule feeds and found that one of the ships getting ready to launch was a bot-driven cargo transport. I plugged into its access from the stationside lock, and greeted it. It could have ignored me, but it was bored, and greeted me back and opened its feed for me. Bots that are also ships don't talk in words. I pushed the thought toward it that I was a happy servant bot who needed a ride to rejoin its beloved guardian, and did it want company on its long trip? I showed it how many hours of shows and books and other media I had saved to share.

Cargo transport bots also watch the entertainment feeds, it turns out.

I don't know what I want. I said that at some point, I think. But it isn't that, it's that I don't want anyone to tell me what I want, or to make decisions for me.

That's why I left you, Dr. Mensah, my favorite human. By the time you get this I'll be leaving Corporation Rim. Out of inventory and out of sight.

Murderbot end message.

Artificial Condition

Chapter One

SECUNITS DON'T CARE ABOUT the news. Even after I hacked my governor module and got access to the feeds, I never paid much attention to it. Partly because downloading the entertainment media was less likely to trigger any alarms that might be set up on satellite and station networks; political and economic news was carried on different levels, closer to the protected data exchanges. But mostly because the news was boring and I didn't care what humans were doing to each other as long as I didn't have to a) stop it or b) clean up after it.

But as I crossed the transit ring's mall, a recent newsburst from Station was in the air, bouncing from one public feed to another. I skimmed it but most of my attention was on getting through the crowd while pretending to be an ordinary augmented human, and not a terrifying murderbot. This involved not panicking when anybody accidentally made eye contact with me.

Fortunately, the humans and augmented humans were too busy trying to get wherever they were going or searching the feed for directions and transport schedules.

Three passenger transports had come through worm-
holes along with the bot-driven cargo transport I had
hitched a ride on, and the big mall between the different
embarkation zones was crowded. Besides the humans,
there were bots of all different shapes and sizes, drones
buzzing along above the crowd, and cargo moving on the
overhead walkways. The security drones wouldn't be
scanning for SecUnits unless they were specifically in-
structed, and nothing had tried to ping me so far, which
was a relief.

I was off the company's inventory, but this was still the
Corporation Rim, and I was still property.

Though I was feeling pretty great about how well I was
doing so far, considering this was only the second transit ring I had been through. SecUnits were shipped to our
contracts as cargo, and we never went through the parts
of stations or transit rings that were meant for people. I'd
had to leave my armor behind in the deployment center
on Station, but in the crowd I was almost as anonymous
as if I was still wearing it. (Yes, that is something I had to
keep repeating to myself.) I was wearing gray and black
work clothes, the long sleeves of the T-shirt and jacket,
the pants and boots covering all my inorganic parts, and
I was carrying a knapsack. Among the varied and colorful clothes, hair, skin, and interfaces of the crowd, I didn't
stand out. The dataport in the back of my neck was visible

but the design was too close to the interfaces augmented humans often had implanted to draw any suspicion. Also, nobody thinks a murderbot is going to be walking along the transit mall like a person.

Then in my skim of the news broadcast I hit an image. It was me.

I didn't stop in my tracks because I have a lot of practice in not physically reacting to things no matter how much they shock or horrify me. I may have lost control of my expression for a second; I was used to always wearing a helmet and keeping it opaqued whenever possible.

I passed a big archway that led to several different food service counters and stopped near the opening to a small business district. Anyone who saw me would assume I was scanning their sites in the feed, looking for information.

The image in the newsburst was of me standing in the lobby of the station hotel with Pin-Lee and Ratthi. The focus was on Pin-Lee, on her determined expression, the annoyed tilt of her eyebrows, and her sharp business clothes. Ratthi and I, in gray PreservationAux survey uniforms, were faded into the background. I was listed as "and bodyguard" in the image tags, which was a relief, but I was braced for the worst as I replayed the story.

Huh, the station I had thought of as The Station, the location of the company offices and the deployment center where I was usually stored, was actually called Port FreeCommerce. I didn't know that. (When I was there, I was mostly in a repair cubicle, a transport box, or in standby waiting for a contract.) The news narrator mentioned in passing how Dr. Mensah had bought the SecUnit who saved her. (That was clearly the heart-warming note to relieve the otherwise grim story with the high body count.) But the journalists weren't used to seeing SecUnits except in armor, or in a bloody pile of leftover pieces when things went wrong. They hadn't connected the idea of a purchased SecUnit with what they assumed was the generic augmented human person going into the hotel with Pin-Lee and Ratthi. That was good.

The weird part was that some of our security recordings had been released. My vantage point, as I searched the DeltFall habitat and found the bodies. Views from Gurathin's and Pin-Lee's helmet cameras, when they found Mensah and what was left of me after the explosion. I scanned through it quickly, making sure there weren't any good views of my human face.

The rest of the story was about how the company and DeltFall, plus Preservation and three other non-corporate political entities who had had citizens in DeltFall's habitat, were ganging up on GrayCris. There was also a multi-cornered solicitor-fight going on in which some of the entities who were allies in the investigation were fighting each other over financial responsibility, jurisdiction, and bond guarantees. I didn't know how humans could keep it all straight. There weren't many details about what had actually happened after PreservationAux had managed to signal the company rescue transport, but it was enough to hope that anybody looking for the SecUnit in question would assume I was with Mensah and the others. Mensah and the others, of course, knew different.

Then I checked the timestamp and saw the newsburst was old, published the cycle after I had left the station. It must have come through a wormhole with one of the faster passenger transports. That meant the official news channels might have more recent info by now.

Right. I told myself there was no way anybody on this transit ring would be looking for a rogue SecUnit. From the info available in the public feed, there were no deployment centers here for any bond or security companies. My contracts had always been on isolated installations or uninhabited survey planets, and I thought that was pretty much the norm. Even the shows and serials on the entertainment feeds never showed SecUnits contracted to guard offices or cargo warehouses or shipwrights, or any of the other businesses common to transit rings. And all the SecUnits in the media were always in armor, faceless and terrifying to humans.

I merged with the crowd and started down the mall again. I had to be careful going anywhere I might be scanned for weapons, which was all the facilities for purchasing transport, including the little trams that circled the ring. I can hack a weapons scanner, but security protocols suggested that at the passenger facilities there would be a lot of them to deal with the crowds and I could only do so many at once. Plus, I would have to hack the payment system, and that sounded like way more trouble than it was worth at the moment. It was a long walk to the part of the ring for the outgoing bot-driven transports, but it gave me time to tap the entertainment feed and download new media.

On the way to this transit ring, alone on my empty cargo transport, I had had a chance to do a lot of thinking about why I had left Mensah, and what I wanted. I know, it was a surprise to me, too. But even I knew I couldn't spend the rest of my lifespan alone riding cargo transports and consuming media, as attractive as it sounded.

I had a plan now. Or I would have a plan, once I got the answer to an important question.

To get that answer I needed to go somewhere, and there were two bot-driven transports leaving here in the next cycle that would take me there. The first was a cargo transport not unlike the one I had used to get here. It was leaving later, and was a better option, as I would have more time to get to it and talk it into letting me board. I could hack a transport if I tried, but I really preferred not to. Spending that much time with something that didn't want you there, or that you had hacked to make it think it wanted you there, just seemed creepy.

Maps and schedules were available in the feed, tied to all the main navigation points along the ring, so I was able to find my way down to the cargo loading area, wait for the shift change, and cut through to the embarkation zone. I had to hack an ID-screening system and some weapon-scanning drones on the level above the zone, and then got pinged by a bot guarding the entrance to the commercial area. I didn't hurt it, just broke through its wall in the feed and deleted out of its memory any record of the encounter with me.

(I was designed to interface with company SecSystems, to be basically an interactive component of one. The safeguards on this station weren't the company's proprietary tech, but it was close enough. Also, nobody is as paranoid as the company about protecting the data it collects and/or steals, so I was used to security systems that were a lot more robust than this.)

Once down on the access floor, I had to be extremely careful, as there was no reason for someone not working to be here, and while most of the work was being done by hauler bots, there were uniformed humans and augmented humans here, too. More than I had counted on.

A lot of humans congregated near the lock for my prospective transport. I checked the feed for alerts and found there had been an accident involving a hauler. Various parties were sorting out the damage and who was to blame. I could have waited until they cleared out, but I wanted to get off this ring and get moving. And honestly, my image in the newsburst had rattled me and I wanted to just sink into my media downloads for a while and pretend I didn't exist. To do that I had to be secure on a locked automated transport ready to leave the ring.

I checked the maps again for my second possibility. It was attached to a different dock, one marked for private, non-commercial traffic. If I moved fast, I could get there before it left.

The schedule had it designated as a long-range research vessel. That sounded like something that would have a crew and probably passengers, but the attached info said it was bot-driven and currently tasked with a cargo run that would stop at the destination I wanted. I had done a historical search in the feed for its movements and found it was owned by a university based on a planet in this system, which rented it out for cargo trips in between assignments to help pay for its upkeep. The trip to my destination would take twenty-one cycles, and I was really looking forward to the isolation.

Getting into the private docks from the commercial docks was easy. I got control of the security system long enough to tell it not to notice that I didn't have authorization, and walked through behind a group of passengers and crew members.

I found the research transport's dock, and pinged it through the comm port. It pinged back almost immediately. All the info I had managed to pull off the feed said it was prepared for an automated run, but just to be sure I sent a hail for attention from human crew. The answer came back a null, no one home.

I pinged the transport again and gave it the same offer I had given the first transport: hundreds of hours of media, serials, books, music, including some new shows I had just picked up on the way through the transit mall, in exchange for a ride. I told it I was a free bot, trying to get back to its human guardian. (The "free bot" thing is deceptive. Bots are considered citizens in some noncorporate political entities like Preservation, but they still have appointed human guardians. Constructs sometimes fall under the same category as bots, sometimes under the same category as deadly weapons. (FYI, that is not a good category to be in.)) This is why I had been a free agent among humans for less than seven cycles, including time spent alone on a cargo transport, and I already needed a vacation.

There was a pause, then the research transport sent an acceptance and opened the lock for me.

Chapter Two

I WAITED TO MAKE sure the lock cycled closed, and that there were no alarms from the ringside, then went down the access corridor. From the schematic available in the shipboard feed, the compartments the transport was using for cargo were normally modular lab space. With the labs sealed and removed to the university's dock storage, there was plenty of room for cargo. I pushed my condensed packet of media into the transport's feed for it to take whenever it wanted.

The rest of the space was the usual engineering, supply storage, cabins, medical, mess hall, with the addition of a larger recreation area and some teaching suites. There was blue and white padding on the furniture and it had all been cleaned recently, though it still had a trace of that dirty sock smell that seems to hang around all human habitations. It was quiet, except for the faint noise of the air system, and my boots weren't making any sound on the deck covering.

I didn't need supplies. My system is self-regulating; I don't need food, water, or to eliminate fluids or solids, and

I don't need much air. I could have lasted on the minimal life support that was all that was provided when no people were aboard, but the transport had upped it a little. I thought that was nice of it.

I wandered around, visually checking things out to see that it matched the schematic, and just making sure everything was okay. I did it, even knowing that patrolling was a habit I was going to have to get over. There were a lot of things I was going to have to get over.

When constructs were first developed, they were originally supposed to have a pre-sentient level of intelligence, like the dumber variety of bot. But you can't put something as dumb as a hauler bot in charge of security for anything without spending even more money for expensive company-employed human supervisors. So they made us smarter. The anxiety and depression were side effects.

In the deployment center, when I was standing there while Dr. Mensah explained why she didn't want to rent me as part of the bond guarantee agreement, she had called the increase in intelligence a "hellish compromise."

This ship was not my responsibility and there were no human clients aboard that I had to keep anything from hurting, or keep from hurting themselves, or keep from hurting each other. But this was a nice ship with surprisingly little security, and I wondered why the owners didn't leave a few humans aboard to keep an eye on it. Like most bot-driven transports, the schematics said there were drones onboard to make repairs, but still.

I kept patrolling until I felt the rumble and clunk through the deck that meant the ship had just decoupled itself from the ring and started to move. The tension that had kept me down to 96 percent capacity eased; a murderbot's life is stressful in general, but it would be a long time before I got used to moving through human spaces with no armor, no way to hide my face.

I found a crew meeting area below the control deck and planted myself in one of the padded chairs. Repair cubicles and transport boxes don't have padding, so traveling in comfort was still a novelty. I started sorting through the new media I'd downloaded on the transit ring. It had some entertainment channels that weren't available on the company's portion of Port FreeCommerce, and they included a lot of new dramas and action series.

I'd never really had long periods of unobserved free time before. The leisure to sort through everything and get it organized, and give it my full attention, without having to monitor multiple systems and the clients' feeds, was still something I was getting used to. Before this, I'd either been on duty, on call, or stuck in a cubicle on standby waiting to be activated for a contract.

I chose a new serial that looked interesting (the tags promised extragalactic exploration, action, and mysteries) and started the first episode. I was ready to settle in until it was time to think about what I was going to do when I got to my destination, something I intended to put off until the last possible moment. Then, through my feed, something said, *You were lucky.*

I sat up. It was so unexpected, I had an adrenaline release from my organic parts.

Transports don't talk in words, even through the feed. They use images and strings of data to alert you to problems, but they're not designed for conversation. I was okay with that, because I wasn't designed for conversation, either. I had shared my stored media with the first transport, and it had given me access to its comm and feed streams so I could make sure no one knew where I was, and that had been the extent of our interaction.

I poked cautiously through the feed, wondering if I'd been fooled. I had the ability to scan, but without drones my range was limited, and with all the shielding and equipment around me I couldn't pick up anything but background readings from the ship's systems. Whoever owned the ship wanted to allow for proprietary research;

the only security cameras were on the hatches, nothing in the crew areas. Or nothing I could access. But the presence in the feed was too big and diffuse for a human or augmented human, I could tell that much even through the feed walls protecting it. And it sounded like a bot. When humans speak in the feed, they have to subvocalize and their mental voice tends to sound like their physical voice. Even augmented humans with full interfaces do it.

Maybe it was trying to be friendly and was just awkward at communicating. I said aloud, "Why am I lucky?"

That no one realized what you were.

That was less than reassuring. I said, cautiously, "What do you think I am?" If it was hostile, I didn't have a lot of options. Transport bots don't have bodies, other than the ship. The equivalent of its brain would be above me, near the bridge where the human flight crew would be stationed. And it wasn't like I had anywhere to go; we were moving out from the ring and making leisurely progress toward the wormhole.

It said, *You're a rogue SecUnit, a bot/human construct, with a scrambled governor module.* It poked me through the feed and I flinched. It said, *Do not attempt to hack my systems,* and for .00001 of a second it dropped its wall.

It was enough time for me to get a vivid image of what I was dealing with. Part of its function was extragalactic astronomic analysis and now all that processing power sat idle while it hauled cargo, waiting for its next mission. It could have squashed me like a bug through the feed, pushed through my wall and other defenses and stripped my memory. Probably while also plotting its wormhole jump, estimating the nutrition needs of a full crew complement for the next 66,000 hours, performing multiple neural surgeries in the medical suite, and beating the captain at tavla. I had never directly interacted with anything this powerful before.

You made a mistake, Murderbot, a really bad mistake. How the hell was I supposed to know there were transports sentient enough to be mean? There were evil bots on the entertainment feed all the time, but that wasn't real, it was just a scary story, a fantasy.

I'd *thought* it was a fantasy.

I said, "Okay," shut down my feed, and huddled down into the chair.

I'm not normally afraid of things, the way humans are. I've been shot hundreds of times, so many times I stopped keeping count, so many times the company stopped keeping count. I've been chewed on by hostile fauna, run over by heavy machinery, tortured by clients for amusement, memory purged, etc., etc. But the inside of my head had been my own for +33,000 hours and I was used to it now. I wanted to keep me the way I was.

The transport didn't respond. I tried to come up with countermeasures for all the different ways it could hurt me and how I could hurt it back. It was more like a Sec-Unit than a bot, so much so I wondered if it was a construct, if there was cloned organic brain tissue buried in its systems somewhere. I'd never tried to hack another SecUnit. It might be safest to go into standby for the duration of the trip, and trigger myself to wake when we reached my destination. Though that would leave me vulnerable to its drones.

I watched seconds click by, waiting to see if it reacted. I was glad I had noted the lack of cameras and not bothered trying to hack into the ship's security system. I understood now why the humans felt it didn't need additional protection. A bot with this complete control over its environment and the initiative and freedom to act could repel any attempt to board.

It had opened the hatch for me. It wanted me here.

Uh-oh.

Then it said, *You can continue to play the media.*

I just huddled there warily.

It added, *Don't sulk.*

I was afraid, but that made me irritated enough to show it that what it was doing to me was not exactly new. I sent through the feed, *SecUnits don't sulk. That would trigger punishment from the governor module,* and attached some brief recordings from my memory of what exactly that felt like.

Seconds added up to a minute, then another, then three more. It doesn't sound like much to humans, but for a conversation between bots, or excuse me, between a bot/human construct and a bot, it was a long time.

Then it said, *I'm sorry I frightened you.*

Okay, well. If you think I trusted that apology, you don't know Murderbot. Most likely it was playing a game with me. I said, "I don't want anything from you. I just want to ride to your next destination." I'd explained that earlier, before it opened the hatch for me, but it was worth repeating.

I felt it withdraw back behind its wall. I waited, and let my circulatory system purge the fear-generated chemicals. More time crawled by, and I started to get bored. Sitting here like this was too much like waiting in a cubicle after I'd been activated, waiting for the new clients to take delivery, for the next boring contract. If it was going to destroy me, at least I could get some media in before that happened. I started the new show again, but I was still too upset to enjoy it, so I stopped it and started rewatching an old episode of *Rise and Fall of Sanctuary Moon.*

After three episodes, I was calmer and reluctantly beginning to see the transport's perspective. A SecUnit could cause it a lot of internal damage if it wasn't careful, and rogue SecUnits were not exactly known for lying low and avoiding trouble. I hadn't hurt the last transport I had taken a ride on, but it didn't know that. I didn't understand why it had let me aboard, if it really didn't want to hurt me. I wouldn't have trusted me, if I was a transport.

Maybe it was like me, and it had taken an opportunity because it was there, not because it knew what it wanted.

It was still an asshole, though.

Six episodes later I felt the transport in the feed again, lurking. I ignored it, though it had to know I knew it was there. In human terms, it was like trying to ignore someone large and breathing heavily while they watched your personal display surface over your shoulder. While leaning on you.

———

I watched seven more episodes of *Sanctuary Moon* with it hanging around my feed. Then it pinged me, like I somehow might not know it had been in my feed all this time, and sent me a request to go back to the new adventure show I had started to watch when it had interrupted me.

(It was called *Worldhoppers,* and was about freelance explorers who extended the wormhole and ring networks into uninhabited star systems. It looked very unrealistic and inaccurate, which was exactly what I liked.)

"I gave you a copy of all my media when I came aboard," I said. I wasn't going to talk to it through the feed like it was my client. "Did you even look at it?"

I examined it for viral malware and other hazards.

And fuck you, I thought, and went back to *Sanctuary Moon*.

Two minutes later it repeated the ping and the request. I said, "Watch it yourself."

I tried. I can process the media more easily through your filter.

That made me stop. I didn't understand the problem.

It explained, *When my crew plays media, I can't process the context. Human interactions and environments outside my hull are largely unfamiliar.*

Now I understood. It needed to read my reactions to the show to really understand what was happening. Humans used the feed in different ways than bots (and constructs) so when its crew played their media, their reactions didn't become part of the data.

I found it odd that the transport was less interested in *Sanctuary Moon,* which took place on a colony, than *Worldhoppers,* which was about the crew of a large exploration ship. You'd think it would be too much like work—I avoided serials about survey teams and mining installations—but maybe familiar things were easier for it.

I was tempted to say no. But if it needed me to watch the show it wanted, then it couldn't get angry and destroy my brain. Also, I wanted to watch the show, too.

"It's not realistic," I told it. "It's not supposed to be realistic. It's a story, not a documentary. If you complain about that, I'll stop watching."

I will refrain from complaint, it said. (Imagine that in the most sarcastic tone you can, and you'll have some idea of how it sounded.)

So we watched *Worldhoppers*. It didn't complain about the lack of realism. After three episodes, it got agitated whenever a minor character was killed. When a major character died in the twentieth episode I had to pause seven minutes while it sat there in the feed doing the bot equivalent of staring at a wall, pretending that it had to run diagnostics. Then four episodes later the character came back to life and it was so relieved we had to watch that episode three times before it would go on.

At the climax of one of the main story lines, the plot suggested the ship might be catastrophically damaged and members of the crew killed or injured, and the transport was afraid to watch it. (That's obviously not how it phrased it, but yeah, it was afraid to watch it.) I was feeling a lot more charitable toward it by that point so was willing to let it ease into the episode by watching one to two minutes at a time.

After it was over, it just sat there, not even pretending to do diagnostics. It sat there for a full ten minutes, which is a lot of processing time for a bot that sophisticated. Then it said, *Again, please.*

So I started the first episode again.

———————

After two more run-throughs of *Worldhoppers,* it wanted to see every other show I had about humans in ships. Though after we encountered one based on a true story, where the ship experienced a hull breach and decompression killed several members of the crew (permanently, this time), it got too upset and I had to create a content filter. To give it a break, I suggested *Sanctuary Moon.* It agreed.

After four episodes, it asked me, *There are no SecUnits in this story?*

It must have thought that *Sanctuary Moon* was my favorite for the same reason that it liked *Worldhoppers.* I said, "No. There aren't that many shows with SecUnits, and they're either villains or the villain's minions." The only SecUnits in entertainment media were rogues, out to kill all humans because they forgot who built the repair cubicles, I guess. In some of the worst shows, Sec-Units would sometimes have sex with the human characters. This was weirdly inaccurate and also anatomically complicated. Constructs with intercourse-related human parts are sexbots, not SecUnits. Sexbots don't have interior weapon systems, so it isn't like it's easy to confuse them with SecUnits. (SecUnits also have less than null interest in human or any other kind of sex, trust me on that.)

Granted, it would have been hard to show realistic SecUnits in visual media, which would involve depicting hours of standing around in brain-numbing boredom, while your nervous clients tried to pretend you weren't there. But there weren't any depictions of SecUnits in books, either. I guess you can't tell a story from the point of view of something that you don't think has a point of view.

It said, *The depiction is unrealistic.*

(You know, just imagine everything it says in the most sarcastic tone possible.)

"There's unrealistic that takes you away from reality and unrealistic that reminds you that everybody's afraid of you." In the entertainment feed, SecUnits were what the clients expected: heartless killing machines that could go rogue at any second, for no reason, despite the governor modules.

The transport thought that over for 1.6 seconds. In a less sarcastic tone, it said, *You dislike your function. I don't understand how that is possible.*

Its function was traveling through what it thought of as the endlessly fascinating sensation of space, and keeping all its human and otherwise passengers safe inside its metal body. Of course it didn't understand not wanting to perform your function. Its function was great.

"I like parts of my function." I liked protecting people and things. I liked figuring out smart ways to protect people and things. I liked being right.

Then why are you here? You are not a "free bot" looking for your guardian, who presumably cannot simply be sent a message via the public comm relay on the transit ring we recently departed.

The question caught me by surprise, because I hadn't thought it was interested in anything besides itself. I hesitated, but it already knew I was a SecUnit, and it already knew there was just no circumstance where it was legal and okay that I was here. It might as well know who I was. I sent my copy of the Port FreeCommerce newsburst into the feed. "That's me."

Dr. Mensah of PreservationAux purchased you and allowed you to leave?

"Yes. Do you want to watch *WorldHoppers* again?" I

regretted the question an instant later. It knew that was an attempt at a distraction.

But it said, *I am not allowed to accept unauthorized passengers or cargo, and have had to alter my log to hide any evidence of your presence.* There was a hesitation. *So we both have a secret.*

I had no reason not to tell it, except fear of sounding stupid. "I left without permission. She offered me a home with her on Preservation, but she doesn't need me there. They don't need SecUnits there. And I . . . didn't know what I wanted, if I wanted to go to Preservation or not. If I want a human guardian, which is just a different word for owner. I knew it would be easier to escape from the station than it would from a planet. So I left. Why did you let me onboard?"

I thought maybe I could distract it by getting it to talk about itself. Wrong again. It said, *I was curious about you, and cargo runs are tedious without passengers. You left to travel to RaviHyral Mining Facility Q Station. Why?*

"I left to get off Port FreeCommerce, away from the company." It waited. "After I had a chance to think, I decided to go to RaviHyral. I need to research something, and that's the best place to do it."

I thought the mention of research might stop its questions, since it understood research. No, not so much. *There were public library feeds available on the transit ring, with* information exchange to the planetary archives. Why not do the research there? My onboard archives are extensive. Why haven't you sought access to them?

I didn't answer. It waited thirty whole seconds, then it said, *The systems of constructs are inherently inferior to advanced bots, but you aren't stupid.*

Yeah, well, fuck you, too, I thought, and initiated a shutdown sequence.

Chapter Three

I JOLTED AWAKE FOUR hours later, when my automatic recharge cycle started. The transport said immediately, *That was unnecessarily childish.*

"What do you know about children?" I was even more angry now because it was right. The shutdown and the time I had spent inert would have driven off or distracted a human; the transport had just waited to resume the argument.

My crew complement includes teachers and students. I have accumulated many examples of childishness.

I just sat there, fuming. I wanted to go back to watching media, but I knew it would think it meant I was giving in, accepting the inevitable. For my entire existence, at least the parts I could remember, I had done nothing but accept the inevitable. I was tired of it.

We are friends now. I don't understand why you won't discuss your plans.

It was such an astonishing, infuriating statement. "We aren't friends. The first thing you did when we were underway was threaten me," I pointed out.

I needed to make certain you didn't attempt to harm me.

I noticed it had said "attempt" and not "intend." If it had cared anything about my intentions it wouldn't have let me onboard in the first place. It had enjoyed showing me it was more powerful than a SecUnit.

Not that it was wrong about the "attempt." While watching the episodes I had managed to do some analysis of it, using the schematics in its own public feed and the specs of similar transports available on the unsecured sections of its database. I had figured out twenty-seven different ways to render it inoperable and three to blow it up. But a mutually assured destruction scenario was not something I was interested in.

If I got through this intact, I needed to find a nicer, dumber transport for the next ride.

I hadn't responded and I knew by now it couldn't stand that. It said, *I apologized.* I still didn't respond. It added, *My crew always considers me trustworthy.*

I shouldn't have let it watch all those episodes of *Worldhoppers.* "I'm not your crew. I'm not a human. I'm a construct. Constructs and bots can't trust each other."

It was quiet for ten precious seconds, though I could tell from the spike in its feed activity it was doing something. I realized it must be searching its databases, looking for a way to refute my statement. Then it said, *Why not?*

I had spent so much time pretending to be patient with humans asking stupid questions. I should have more self-control than this. "Because we both have to follow human orders. A human could tell you to purge my memory. A human could tell me to destroy your systems."

I thought it would argue that I couldn't possibly hurt it, which would derail the whole conversation.

But it said, *There are no humans here now.*

I realized I had been trapped into this conversational dead end, with the transport pretending to need this explained in order to get me to articulate it to myself. I didn't know who I was more annoyed at, myself or it. No, I was definitely more annoyed at it.

I sat there for a while, wanting to go back to the media, any media, rather than think about this. I could feel it in the feed, waiting, watching me with all its attention except for the miniscule amount of awareness it needed to keep itself on course.

Did it really matter if it knew? Was I afraid knowing would change its opinion of me? (As far as I could tell, its opinion was already pretty low.) Did I really care what an asshole research transport thought about me?

I shouldn't have asked myself that question. I felt a wave of non-caring about to come over me, and I knew I couldn't let it. If I was going to follow my plan, such as it was, I needed to care. If I let myself not care, then there was no telling where I'd end up. Riding dumb transports watching media until somebody caught me and sold me back to the company, probably, or killed me for my inorganic parts.

I said, "At some point approximately 35,000 hours ago, I was assigned to a contract on RaviHyral Mining Facility Q Station. During that assignment, I went rogue and killed a large number of my clients. My memory of the incident was partially purged." SecUnit memory purges are always partial, due to the organic parts inside our heads. The purge can't wipe memory from organic neural tissue. "I need to know if the incident occurred due to a catastrophic failure of my governor module. That's what I think happened. But I need to know for sure." I hesitated, but what the hell, it already knew everything else. "I need to know if I hacked my governor module in order to cause the incident."

I don't know what I expected. I knew ART (aka Asshole Research Transport) had a deeper attachment to its crew than SecUnits had for clients. If it didn't feel that way about the humans it carried and worked with, then it wouldn't have gotten so upset whenever anything happened to the characters on *Worldhoppers*. I wouldn't have had to filter out all the based-on-a-true-story shows where human crews got hurt. I knew what it felt, because I felt that way about Mensah and PreservationAux.

It said, *Why was your memory of the incident purged?*

That wasn't the question I was expecting. "Because SecUnits are expensive and the company didn't want to lose any more money on me than it already had." I wanted to fidget. I wanted to say something so offensive to it that it would leave me alone. I really wanted to stop thinking about this and watch *Sanctuary Moon*. "Either I killed them due to a malfunction and then hacked the governor module, or I hacked the governor module so I could kill them," I said. "Those are the only two possibilities."

Are all constructs so illogical? said the Asshole Research Transport with the immense processing capability whose metaphorical hand I had had to hold because it had become emotionally compromised by a fictional media serial. Before I could say that, it added, *Those are not the first two possibilities to consider.*

I had no idea what it meant. "All right, what are the first two possibilities to consider?"

That it either happened, or it didn't.

———————

I had to get up and pace.

Ignoring me, ART continued, *If it happened, did you cause it to happen, or did an outside influence use you to*

cause it to happen? If an outside influence caused it to happen, why? Who benefited from the incident?

ART seemed happy to have the problem laid out so
clearly. I wasn't sure I was. "I know I could have hacked
my governor module." I pointed at my head. "Hacking my
governor module is why I'm here."

*If your ability to hack your governor module was what
caused the incident, why was it not checked periodically and
the current hack detected?*

There would be no point in hacking the module if I
couldn't fool the standard diagnostics. But . . . The company was cheap and sloppy, but not stupid. I had been
kept in a deployment center attached to corporate offices.
So they hadn't anticipated any potential danger.

ART said, *You are correct that further research is called
for before the incident can be understood fully. How do you
plan to proceed?*

I stopped pacing. It knew how I planned to proceed.
Go to RaviHyral, look for information. There hadn't been
anything in the company's knowledge base that I could
access without getting caught, but the systems on Ravi-
Hyral itself might not be so well protected. And maybe
if I saw the place again, it would spark something in my
human neural tissue. (I wasn't much looking forward to
that part, if it happened.) I could tell ART was doing that
thing again where it asked me questions it knew the an-

swer to so it could trap me into admitting stuff that I
didn't want to admit. I decided to just skip to the end.
"What do you mean?"

You will be identified as a SecUnit.

That stung a little. "I can pass as an augmented human."
Augmented humans are still considered humans. I don't
know if there are any augmented humans with enough
implants to resemble a SecUnit. It seems unlikely a
human would want that many implants, or would survive
whatever catastrophic injury might make them necessary. But humans are weird. Whatever, I didn't intend to
let anyone see more than I absolutely had to.

You look like a SecUnit. You move like a SecUnit. It sent
a whole array of images into the feed, comparing a recording of me moving around its corridors and cabins with
recordings of various members of its crew in the same
spaces. I had relaxed, relieved to be off the transit ring,
but I didn't look very relaxed. I looked like a patrolling
SecUnit.

"No one noticed on the transit rings," I said. I knew I
was taking a chance. I had gotten by so far because the
humans and augmented humans in the commercial
transport rings didn't see SecUnits except on the entertainment feed or in the news, where we were mostly killing people or already blasted into pieces. If I was spotted
by anyone who had ever worked a long-term contract

with SecUnits, there was a good chance they would realize what I was.

ART brought up a map listing. The RaviHyral Mining
Facility Q Station was the third largest moon of a gas
giant. The map rotated, with the various mining installations and support centers and the port highlighted.
There was only the one port. *These installations will
employ SecUnits/have employed SecUnits. You will be seen
by human authorities who have worked with SecUnits.*

I hate it when ART is right. "I can't do anything about
that."

You can't alter your configuration.

I could see the skepticism through the feed. "No, I
can't. Look up the specs on SecUnits."

SecUnits are never altered. Skepticism intensifying. It
had obviously pulled all the information on SecUnits in
its database and assimilated it.

"No. Sexbots are altered." At least the ones I had seen
had been altered. Some were mostly Unit standard with
a few changes, others were radically different. "But that's
done in the deployment center, in the repair cubicles. To
do anything like that I'd need a medical suite. A full one,
not just an emergency kit."

It said, *I have a full medical suite. Alterations can be made
there.*

That was true, but even a medical suite as good as what

ART had, able to carry out thousands of unassisted procedures on humans, wouldn't have the programming to physically alter a SecUnit. I might be able to guide it through the process, but there was a big problem with that. Alterations to my organic and nonorganic components would cause catastrophic function loss if I wasn't deactivated when they took place. "Theoretically. But I can't operate the medical suite while I'm being altered."

I can.

I didn't say anything. I started sorting through my media again.

Why are you not responding?

I knew ART well enough by now to know it wouldn't leave me alone, so I went ahead and spelled it out. "You want me to trust you to alter my configuration while I'm inactive? When I'm helpless?"

It had the audacity to sound offended. *I assist my crew in many procedures.*

I got up, paced, stared at the bulkhead for two minutes, then ran a diagnostic. Finally, I said, "Why do you want to help me?"

I'm accustomed to assisting my crew with large-scale data analysis, and numerous other experiments. While I am in transport mode, I find my unused capacity tiresome. Solving your problems is an interesting exercise in lateral thinking.

"So you're bored? I'd be the best toy you've ever had?"

When I was on inventory, I would have given anything for twenty-one cycles of unobserved downtime. I couldn't feel sorry for ART. "If you're bored, watch the media I gave you."

I am aware that for you, your survival as a rogue Unit would be at stake.

I started to correct it, then stopped. Rogue was not how I thought of myself. I had hacked my governor module but continued to obey orders, at least most of them. I had not escaped from the company; Dr. Mensah had legally bought me. While I had left the hotel without her permission, she hadn't told me not to leave, either. (Yes, I know the last one isn't helping the argument all that much.)

Rogue units killed their human and augmented human clients. I . . . had done that once. But not voluntarily.

I needed to find out whether or not it had been voluntary.

"My survival isn't at stake if I continue to ride unoccupied transports." And learn to avoid the asshole ones that want to threaten me and question all my choices and try to talk me into getting into the medical suite so they could do experimental surgery on me.

Is that all you want? You don't want to return to your crew?

I said, not patiently, "I don't have a crew."

It sent me an image from the newsburst I had given it, a group image of PreservationAux. Everybody was in their gray uniforms, smiling, for a team portrait taken at the start of the contract. *That isn't your crew?*

I didn't know how to answer it.

I had spent thousands of hours watching or reading about, and liking, groups of fictional humans in the media. Then I had ended up with a group of real humans to watch and like, and then somebody tried to kill them, and while protecting them I had to tell them I had hacked my governor module. So I left. (Yes, I know it's more complicated than that.)

I tried to think about why I didn't want to change my configuration, even to help protect myself. Maybe because it was something humans did to sexbots. I was a murderbot, I had to have higher standards?

I didn't want to look more human than I already did. Even when I was still in armor, once my PreservationAux clients had seen my human face, they had wanted to treat me like a person. Make me ride in the crew section of the hopper, bring me in for their strategy meetings, talk to me. About my feelings. I couldn't take that.

But I didn't have the armor anymore. My appearance, my ability to pass as an augmented human, had to be my new armor. It wouldn't work if I couldn't pass among humans who were familiar with SecUnits.

But that seemed pointless, and I felt another wave of "I don't care" coming on. Why should I care? I liked humans, I liked watching them on the entertainment feed, where they couldn't interact with me. Where it was safe. For me and for them.

If I had gone back to Preservation with Dr. Mensah and the others, she might be able to guarantee my safety, but could I really guarantee her safety from me?

Altering my physical configuration still seemed drastic. But hacking my governor module was drastic. Leaving Dr. Mensah was drastic.

ART said, almost plaintively, *I don't understand why this is a difficult choice.*

I didn't, either, but I wasn't going to tell it that.

———

I took two cycles to think it over. I didn't talk to ART about it, or anything else, though we kept watching media together, and it exercised a self-restraint I didn't think it had and didn't try to start arguments with me.

I knew I had been lucky up to this point. Onboard the transport I had used to leave Port FreeCommerce, I had compared myself to recordings of humans, trying to isolate what factors might cause me to be identified as a SecUnit. The most correctable behavior was restless movement. Humans and augmented humans shift their weight when they stand, they react to sudden sounds and bright lights, they scratch themselves, they adjust their hair, they look in their pockets or bags to check for things that they already know are in there.

SecUnits don't move. Our default is to stand and stare at the things we're guarding. Partly this is because our non-organic parts don't need movement the way organic parts do. But mostly it's because we don't want to draw attention to ourselves. Any unusual movement might cause a human to think there's something wrong with you, which will draw more scrutiny. If you've gotten stuck with one of the bad contracts, it might cause the humans to order the HubSystem to use your governor module to immobilize you.

After analyzing human movement, I wrote some code for myself, to cause me to make a random series of movements periodically if I was standing still. To change my respiration to react to changes in the air quality. To vary my walking speed, to make sure I reacted to stimuli physically instead of just scanning and noting it. This code had gotten me through the second transit ring. But would I be all right on a ring or installation frequented by humans who often saw or worked with SecUnits?

I tweaked my code a little and asked ART to record me again as I moved around its corridors and compartments.

I tried to make myself look as much like a human as possible. I'm used to feeling mentally awkward around humans, and I took that sensation and tried to express it in my physical movements. I felt pretty good about the result. Until I looked at the recordings and compared them to ART's recordings of its crew and my recordings of other SecUnits.

The only one I was fooling here was myself.

The change in movement made me look more human but my proportions exactly matched the other SecUnits. I was good enough to fool humans who weren't looking for me, since humans tend to ignore non-standard behavior in transitional public spaces. But anyone who had set out to find me, who was alert to the possibility of a rogue SecUnit, might not be fooled, and a simple scan calibrated to search for SecUnit size, height, and weight was certain to find me.

It was the logical choice, it was the obvious choice, and I would still rather peel my human skin off than do it.

I was going to have to do it.

―――――――

After a lot of argument, we agreed the easiest change for the best result was to take two centimeters of length out of my legs and arms. It doesn't sound like a big change, but it meant my physical proportions would no longer match Unit standard. It would change the way I walked, the way I moved. It made sense and I was fine with it.

Then ART said we also needed to change the code controlling my organic parts, so they could grow hair.

My first reaction to that was no fucking way. I had hair on my head, and eyebrows; that was a part of SecUnit configuration that was shared with sexbots, though the code controlling it kept SecUnit head hair short to keep it from interfering with the armor. The whole idea of constructs is that we look human, so we don't make the clients uncomfortable with our appearance. (I could have told the company that the fact that SecUnits are terrifying killing machines does, in fact, make humans nervous regardless of what we look like, but nobody listens to me.) But the rest of my skin was hairless.

I told ART that I preferred it that way and extra hair would just draw unwanted attention. It replied that it meant the fine, sparse hair humans had on parts of their skin. ART had done some analysis and come up with a list of biological features that humans might notice subliminally. Hair was the only one we could change my underlying code to create, and ART proposed that it would make the joins between the organic and inorganic parts on my arms, legs, chest, and back look more like augments, the inorganic parts that humans had implanted for medical or other reasons. I pointed out that many humans or augmented humans had the hair on their bodies removed, for hygienic or cosmetic reasons and because who the hell wants it there anyway. ART countered that humans didn't have to worry about being identified as SecUnits, so they could do whatever they wanted to their bodies.

I still wanted to argue, because I didn't want to agree with anything ART said right now. But it seemed minor in comparison to removing two centimeters of synthetic bone and metal from my legs and arms, and changing the code for how my organic parts would grow around them.

ART had an alternate, more drastic plan that included giving me sex-related parts, and I told it that was absolutely not an option. I didn't have any parts related to sex and I liked it that way. I had seen humans have sex on the entertainment feed and on my contracts, when I had been required to record everything the clients said and did. No, thank you, no. No.

But I did ask it to make an alteration to the dataport in the back of my neck. It was a vulnerable point, and I didn't want to miss the opportunity to take care of it.

Once we agreed on the process, I stood in front of the surgical suite. The MedSystem had just sterilized and prepped itself and there was a heavy scent of antibacterials in the air, reminding me of every time I had carried an injured client into a room like this. I was thinking about all the ways this could go wrong, and the terrible things ART could do to me if it wanted.

ART said, *What is causing the delay? Is there a preliminary process left to complete?*

I had no reason to trust it. Except the way it kept wanting to watch media about humans in ships, and got upset when the violence was too realistic.

I sighed, stripped off my clothes, and laid down on the surgical platform.

Chapter Four

I CAME BACK ONLINE to find I was at 26 percent capacity, but the percentage was climbing slowly. Bands of pain circled my knee and elbow joints, so intense I couldn't process it. My human skin itched. And I was leaking. I hate that.

I didn't have the capacity to access or play any of my media. All I could do was lie there waiting for my levels to adjust. Attempts to move just made it worse. I wished I had gone with Plan Sixteen to render the ART inoperable, the one with the best statistical chance of success without me taking catastrophic damage in retaliation. Plan Two to blow it up was looking pretty attractive at the moment, too. This had been a stupid thing to agree to.

It was like being in a cubicle after being shot to pieces, but without a cubicle's ability to shut down higher functions until the repairs were complete. I had known going in that the MedSystem wouldn't be able to adjust my pain level, but I hadn't thought it would be this bad. I couldn't adjust my own temperature, either, but I wasn't cold, as the MedSystem was controlling the temperature of the room and the platform to keep me at a comfortable level. Cubicles didn't do that and I had to admit it was nice.

Gradually my levels started to even out and I got back enough function to dial down my pain sensor and turn off the itching. I needed some pain to tell me what not to move until all the regrowth of my organic tissue was complete.

ART was hanging around out in my feed but mercifully hadn't tried to talk to me yet. At 75 percent capacity, I tried to sit up.

MedSystem started to throw warnings and ART said, *There is no reason to move now. During the process I ran a search of my onboard public information newsfeed bases during the time period in question, regarding unusual fatalities relating to mining. Do you want my conclusions based on the results?*

I eased back down, feeling my organic parts cling to the warm metal of the platform. I was now leaking from a different spot. I told ART I knew how to fucking read search results.

I would defer to your expertise in shooting and killing things. You should defer to mine in data analysis.

I told it fine, whatever. I didn't think there would be anything useful.

It sent its conclusions into the feed. Admittedly, it made sense that a large number of deaths under unusual circumstances would end up in some sort of public record available to multiple newsfeeds, the way the DeltFall incident had. The RaviHyral incident might have been classed as an accident, but a company bond was involved so there would have been a legal battle. Though if the data said it was a rogue SecUnit who had killed everyone, that didn't give me any more information than I already had.

Records across several archived newsfeeds indicate the site of the incident was likely a small installation called Ganaka Pit. The information originates in a source from Kalidon, a political entity on the Corporation Rim, where the company funding Ganaka Pit was based. There were fifty-seven fatalities. The cause is listed as "equipment failure."

SecUnits were categorized on inventory as equipment.

ART waited, and when I didn't say anything, added, *So your initial assumption was correct, the incident did occur. Investigation can now proceed.*

I wanted to shut down, but it would interfere with the healing process.

ART asked, *Do you wish to watch media?*

I didn't respond, but it started an episode of *Sanctuary Moon* anyway.

———————

When I was finally able to climb off the platform, I fell on the deck, but by the end of that cycle I was almost back to normal. The first thing I did was wash off all the blood and other assorted fluids in the bathing facility attached to the MedSystem bay. Security ready rooms had facilities where I could clean off the blood and fluids after a fight or a repair, but I had never used a facility meant for humans. ART had good ones, with the recycled cleaning fluid that was so much like water it was hard to tell the difference without a chemical analysis. You could adjust the temperature to make it warmer, and it smelled good. I smelled like a clean human afterward, and that was just odd.

The fine hair that was coming up in patches in various places was strange but not as annoying as I had anticipated. It might be inconvenient the next time I had to put on a suit skin, but the humans with hair seemed to manage with a minimum of complaint, so I figured I would, too. The change in code had also made my eyebrows thicker and the hair on my head a few centimeters longer. I could feel it, and it was weird.

I went to ART's rec space and used the treadmill and the other machines to test myself, making sure my weapons were still functioning correctly and my aim wasn't off. (I didn't test fire them, as ART let me know that it would set off the fire protection system if I did.)

I looked at myself in the mirror for a long time.

I told myself I still looked like a SecUnit without armor, hopelessly exposed, but the truth was I did look more human. And now I knew why I hadn't wanted to do this.

It would make it harder for me to pretend not to be a person.

We exited the wormhole on schedule. As soon as we were in range of the transit ring, ART stretched its reception and picked up the destination info packet for me, which included a more detailed map of RaviHyral. Rotating the map to look at it from every angle didn't jog anything in the fragments of memory I had of that time. But it was interesting that Ganaka Pit wasn't marked anywhere.

I could feel ART in my feed, looking over my figurative shoulder again. I checked the timestamp, and saw the map had been updated multiple times since the time period of my incident. "They took it off the map."

Is this usual? ART asked. It dealt only with star maps, and removing something from one of those was kind of a big deal.

"I don't know if it's usual or not, but it makes sense, if the company or the clients wanted to conceal what happened." If the company wanted to continue to sell contracts for SecUnits to other mining installations, concealing the fact, or at least obscuring the fact, that fatalities had occurred was important. Maybe instead of a legal battle, the company had paid out on the bonds quickly under the condition that the client minimize details about the incident in the public record. This hadn't been a situation like GrayCris and DeltFall, where there were multiple parties involved and the company was all over the newsfeeds, trying to generate sympathy for itself.

ART pulled more historical info, searching the pit and service installation names that were listed. RaviHyral had originally been held by a number of companies with mining rights to different areas of the moon's interior. But over the past two system-years, a company called Umro had bought out some of the claims, though many of the original companies were still operating as contractors. None of the names sounded familiar.

I'd have to figure out where Ganaka Pit had been before I could go there. I would have been transported there as freight and there weren't any memories of the trip, partially erased or not.

I started to search through the rest of the info packet, looking for schedules. I would have to get a shuttle from the transit ring to the RaviHyral port. That would be tricky. Well, the whole thing would be tricky. From the information on the shipping schedule, only people with employment vouchers or passes from one of the mining installations or support services were allowed to board the shuttles. There was no tourism, nobody coming and going without official authorization from one of the companies or contractors on the moon. Since I wasn't a person and I didn't have an employment voucher, I would have to hack my way into one of the supply shuttles . . .

ART was still pulling data from the station feed. *I have a suggestion,* it told me, and displayed a set of personal advertisements. I had seen these in the feeds at Port FreeCommerce and the last transit ring, but hadn't paid attention. ART highlighted one that was a job listing for a temporary position as security for a technologist group on limited contract.

"What?" I asked ART. I didn't understand why it was showing me this.

If this group hired you, you would have an employment voucher for travel to the installation.

"Hire me." I've had more contracts than I can remember (I mean that literally. A lot of them were before the memory purge) but none of them were voluntary. The company pulled me out of storage, showed me to the client, then packed me into the cargo hold. "Have you lost your mind?"

My crew hires consultants for every voyage. ART was impatient that I wasn't complimenting it yet on its great idea. *The procedure is simple.*

"For humans and augmented humans, yes." I was stalling. I would have to interact with humans as an augmented human. I know that's what altering my configuration was supposed to be for, but I had imagined it as taking place from a distance, or in the spaces of a crowded transit ring. Interacting meant talking, and eye contact. I could already feel my performance capacity dropping.

It will be simple, ART insisted. *I'll assist you.*

Yes, the giant transport bot is going to help the construct SecUnit pretend to be human. This will go well.

———

Once ART was docked and the transit ring's bot-piloted tugs were removing the cargo modules, it cycled the lock for me and I slipped through into the embarkation zone.

It had given me access to its comm so it could ride my feed through the transit ring. It claimed it could help me and while I was skeptical of that, it could at least keep me company. As I walked away from the safety of ART's lock, I dropped back down to 96 percent efficiency. I hit the station entertainment feeds for new downloads to try to calm down.

I'd already sent a message to the social feed node about the advertisement, and gotten an answer with a location and timestamp. The last time I'd had an arranged meeting with humans they kidnapped Mensah and blew me up, so. This could hardly be worse.

I hacked my way through embarkation zone security and out into the ring's mall. It was utilitarian compared to both the last transit ring and Port FreeCommerce. No garden pods, no holo sculptures, no big holo displays advertising arrays of shipwrights and cargo factors and other businesses, no shiny new interface vending machines. Also no big passenger transports coming through, so not nearly as big a crowd, of humans or bots. ART's idea was beginning to seem less like a stupid risk and more like a necessity. Blending in here would be harder, if everyone was only here on their way to and from the installations on the moon. In my feed, ART said, *I told you so.*

The location for the meeting was a food service place

in the main mall area. It was in a large transparent bubble in the second level of the mall, overlooking the walkways and counter service stalls below. There were multiple open levels inside, with tables and chairs, and it was 40 percent full of humans and augmented humans. As I walked through, I picked up the occasional buzz of a drone, but no pings. There were food smells in the air, and the acrid scents of intoxicants. I didn't bother to try to analyze and identify them; I was too nervous and trying to focus on looking like an augmented human.

The humans I was to meet had sent an image so I could find them. There were three of them, all wearing variations on work clothes, no uniform logos. A quick search had shown entries for them in the transit ring's social feed. They had listed themselves as unaffiliated guest workers, but you could list yourself as anything, there was no identity check. Two were female, and one was tercera, which was a gender signifier used in the group of non-corporate political entities known as the Divarti Cluster.

(To initiate the meeting, I'd had to make an entry on the social feed, too. The system was extremely vulnerable to hacking, so I had backdated my entry to look like I had come in on an earlier passenger transport, listed my job as "security consultant," and my gender as indeterminate. Posing as its own captain, ART gave me a prior employment reference.)

I spotted them at a table near the bubble overlooking the mall. They were having a tense whispered conversation and body language said they were nervous. As I walked toward them, my quick scan showed no weapon signatures, just the small power sources of their personal feed interfaces. One had an implant, but it was just a low-level feed access tool.

I had practiced this part with ART on approach to the ring, recording myself so both of us could critique it. I told myself I could do this. I put on my best neutral expression, the one I used when the extra download activity had been detected and the deployment center's supervisor was blaming the human techs for it. I walked up to the table and said, "Hello."

All three of them flinched. "Uh, hello," the tercera said, recovering first.

I picked up the feed from the security camera so I could watch myself and make sure my facial expressions were under control. And it was easier to talk to the humans while watching them through the cameras. I was well aware it was a completely false sensation of distance from the situation, but I needed it. I said, "We arranged to meet. I'm Eden, the security consultant." Right, so, it was the name of one of the characters in *Sanctuary Moon*. You probably aren't surprised by that.

The tercera cleared ter throat. Te had purple hair and

red eyebrows, standing out against light brown skin. "I'm Rami, that's Tapan, and Maro." Te shifted nervously and tapped the empty chair.

ART, who was considerably faster than me at data retrieval, performed a quick search and informed me it was an invitation to sit down across several human cultural indices. It was giving me the etymology of the gesture as I sat down. You would think a SecUnit who had been shot to pieces multiple times, blown up, memory purged, and once partially dismantled by accident wouldn't be on the verge of panic under these circumstances. You'd be wrong.

Rami added, "Uh, I'm not sure where to start." Tapan nudged ter, apparently conveying moral support. Tapan had multicolored braids wrapped up around her head, and a blue jewel-toned interface clipped to her ear, and slightly darker skin than Rami. Maro had very dark skin, and silver-colored little puffs of hair, and was almost beautiful enough to be in the entertainment media. I'm terrible at estimating human ages because it's not one of the few things I care about. Also most of my experience is with the humans on the entertainment feed, and they aren't anything like the ones you see in reality. (One of the many reasons I'm not fond of reality.) But I thought all three might be young. Not children, but maybe not that far from adolescence.

They stared at me, and I realized I was going to have

to help. I said, cautiously, "You want to hire a security consultant?" This was what they had posted on the social feed, and from the number of similar requests, it was common for groups and individuals to hire private security before going to RaviHyral. I guess hiring human security guards is what you do when you can't afford real security.

Rami seemed relieved. "Yes, we need help."

Maro threw a look around and said, "We shouldn't talk here, maybe. Is there someplace else we could go?"

It had been stressful enough getting here, I didn't want to have to go anywhere else right now. I did a quick scan for drones, then initiated a glitch in the connection between the restaurant and transit ring security. I caught the cameras and showed ART what I wanted it to do. It took over and edited me out of the system's recording and cut the camera watching the table out of the system. I unglitched the connection to the ring's main security, which wouldn't notice the missing camera feed for the short time we would be here. I said, "It's all right. We're not being recorded."

They stared at me. Rami said, "But there's security— Did you do something?"

"I'm a security consultant," I repeated. My panic level was starting to drop, primarily because they were so obviously nervous. Humans are nervous of me because I'm a terrifying murderbot, and I'm nervous of them because they're humans. But I knew that humans could also be wary and nervous of each other in non-combat and non-adversarial situations, in reality and not just as part of a story. That was what seemed to be happening, but it let me pretend this was business as usual during one of the rare occasions when clients asked my advice about security.

Part of my job as a SecUnit was to give clients advice when they asked for it, as I was theoretically the one with all the information on security. Not that a lot of them had asked for it, or had listened to me. Not that I'm bitter about that, or anything.

Tapan looked impressed. "So you're spliced, right?" She patted the back of her neck, indicating where my data port was. "You got augments? You have extra access to the feed?"

"Spliced" was an informal term for an augmented human; I'd heard it on the entertainment feed. I said, "Yes." Then added, "Among other things."

Rami's red brows lifted in understanding. Maro looked impressed, and said, "I don't know if we can afford— Our credit account is— If we can get our data back, then—"

Rami took it up again. "Then we would have plenty to pay you."

ART, who was apparently very interested in the job scenario, started to search the public feeds for a pay scale for private security consultants. I reminded myself that I was pretending not to be a SecUnit, so me questioning them wouldn't seem out of the ordinary. I decided to start with the basic information. "Why do you want to hire me?"

Rami looked at the other two, got nods in response, and cleared ter throat. "We were working on Ravi-Hyral, for Tlacey Excavations, one of the smaller Umro contractors. We do mineral research and technology development." Te explained that they were a collective of technologists, seven of them plus dependents, who traveled from work contract to work contract. The others were waiting in a hotel suite, with Rami, Maro, and Tapan having been deputized to act for the group. It was a relief to hear that their mining experience was in tech and research; in the mining contracts I had had, the techs were usually in offices off the pit site or adjacent to it, and we didn't see them unless they got intoxicated and tried to kill each other, which admittedly was rare.

"Tlacey's terms were great," Tapan added, "but maybe too great, if you know what I mean."

ART did a quick search and returned the opinion that it was intended to be a figure of speech. I told it I knew that.

Rami continued, "We took the contract because it would give us time to work on our own stuff. We'd had this idea to develop a new detection system for strange synthetics. RaviHyral has a lot of identified deposits, so it's a great place for research." Strange synthetics were elements left behind by alien civilizations. Telling the difference between them and naturally occurring elements that were previously unidentified was a problem in mining. Like the remnants of alien occupation/civilization uncovered by GrayCris on my last contract, they were off limits for commercial development. That was all I'd ever needed to know, since every job I'd ever had involving alien material was just me standing around guarding the people who were working on it. (ART tried to explain it to me and I told it to save it for later, I needed to focus.)

Rami said, "We were making good progress, but then suddenly our group got terminated with no notice, and they took our data—"

Tapan waved her hands. "All our work! It wasn't anything to do with our contract—"

Maro finished, "Tlacey stole it, basically, and they deleted the most current version off our devices. We had copies of the older iterations, but we've lost all our recent work."

Rami added, "We filed a complaint with Umro, but it's taking forever to process it, and we don't know if it's ever going to come to anything."

I said, "This sounds like something you should go to a

solicitor about." It wasn't unusual. The company data mined, too, but it wasn't as clumsy or obvious as to try to delete the work from the original creators' devices. If it did that, then the creators wouldn't come back and enter into more security bond agreements, which would give the company access to whatever they were working on next.

"We thought about a solicitor," Rami said. "But we aren't in the union, so it would be expensive. But then yesterday Tlacey finally answered our petition, and said we could have the files back if we returned our signing bonus. We have to go down to RaviHyral to do that." Te sat back in ter chair. "That's why we wanted to hire you."

This was starting to make sense. "You don't trust Tlacey."

"We just want somebody on our side," Tapan clarified.

"No, we definitely don't trust Tlacey," Maro countered. "Not at all. We need security for when we get there, if things get . . . touchy. Tlacey herself is supposed to meet us, and she has an entourage of bodyguards, and there's no general security except what Umro has in the public areas and the port, and that's not much."

I didn't know exactly what she thought she meant by "touchy," but all the scenarios I could imagine in that situation weren't good ones.

The company offered SecUnits so the clients didn't

have to hire humans to guard each other. From what I had seen in the serials, me doing a half-assed version of my job was still better than a human trying to do it.

I was still watching us through the captured security camera even though I wasn't allowing it to record. I could see my expression was dubious, but in this case I think the situation warranted it. I said, "The meeting with Tlacey could be held through a secured comm channel." The company bonded those, too, for funds and data transfer.

Maro, whose expression was even more dubious than mine, said, "Yeah, but Tlacey wants to do it in person."

Rami admitted, "We know it doesn't sound like a good idea to go."

It was a great idea to go if you wanted to be murdered. I had hoped for an easier job, courier duty, or something similar. But this was protecting humans who were determined to do something dangerous, which was exactly the kind of job I was designed for. The job that I had kept doing more or less, often as less as possible, even after I had hacked my governor module. I was used to having something useful to do, taking care of something, even if it was only a contractually obligated group of humans who if I was lucky treated me like a tool and not a toy.

After PreservationAux, it had occurred to me how different it would be to do my job as an actual member of the group I was protecting. And that was the main reason I was here.

I phrased it as a question, because pretending you were asking for more information was the best way to try to get the humans to realize they were doing something stupid. "So do you think there's another reason Tlacey wants you to do this exchange in person, other than . . . killing you?"

Tapan grimaced, as if that was something she had been aware of but trying not to think about. Maro tapped the table and pointed at me, which was vaguely alarming until ART identified it as a gesture of emphatic agreement. Rami took a sharp breath and said, "We think . . . We weren't finished, our process was incomplete, but we were so enthusiastic about it . . . We think they must have listened in using the security feeds and heard us talking, and thought we were much further along than we actually were. So I don't know if they can complete it. Maybe they realized it's not worth much without us to finish it."

"Maybe Tlacey wants us to work for her again," Tapan said hopefully.

Probably, before she murders you, I didn't say.

Maro snorted. "I would rather live in a box in a station mall than work for her again."

Once they had started to talk about it, it was hard for them to stop. The collective was completely divided on what to do, which was apparently painful for all of them since they were used to agreeing on everything. Tapan, who according to Maro was too naive for this existence, thought it was worth a try. Maro, who according to Tapan was a cynical impediment to both fun and progress, thought they were screwed and should just cut their losses. Rami was undecided, which was why te had been elected leader of the collective for the duration of this problem. Rami did not seem thrilled by the collective's confidence, but was gamely trying to proceed.

Finally, Rami finished up with, "So that's why we want to hire you. We thought it would be better to go in with someone who could protect us, keep her crew from messing with us, show her we have backup while we negotiate."

What they needed was a security company willing to bond them for the meeting and return trip, and send a SecUnit with them to guarantee their safety. But security companies like that are expensive, and wouldn't be interested in a job this small.

They all stared at me worriedly. In the security camera view, from that angle, it was obvious how small they were. They looked so soft, with all the fluffy multicolored hair. And nervous, but not of me. I said, "I accept your job."

Rami and Tapan looked relieved, and Maro, who clearly still didn't want to do this, looked resigned. She said, "How much do we pay you?" She glanced uncertainly at the others. "Can we afford you, I mean."

ART had a set of spreadsheets ready but I didn't want to scare them off with a figure that was too high. "How much were they paying you before you were terminated?"

Rami said, "It's two hundred CRs per cycle for each worker for the limited term of contract."

It didn't sound like this would take more than a cycle. "You can pay me that."

"One cycle's share of the contract?" Rami sat up straight. "Really?"

Ter reaction meant I'd asked for far too little, but it was too late to correct the mistake. I did need to give them a reason why I was willing to settle for a small amount, and I decided the partial truth was better. "I need to go to RaviHyral, and I need an employment contract to get there."

"Why?" Tapan asked, and Rami nudged her by way of admonishment. "I mean, I know we don't have a right to ask, but . . ."

Don't have a right to ask. That wasn't something that had ever applied to me, before PreservationAux. I told the truth again. "I need to do some research there for another client."

Like ART, they understood the idea of research, especially proprietary research, and they didn't ask any

Chapter Five

I MET THEM AT the embarkation zone. I had the knapsack, which was part of my human disguise, but the only important thing I was carrying was the comm interface from ART. It would allow us to communicate once I was down on RaviHyral and let me continue to have access to ART's knowledge bases and unsolicited opinions. I was used to having a HubSystem and a SecSystem for backup and ART would be taking their place. (Without the part where those two systems were partly designed to rat me out to the company and trigger punishment through the governor module. ART's freedom to weigh in on everything I did was punishment enough.) I had inserted the comm interface in a built-in compartment under my ribs.

All three of my clients were waiting, each with a small bag or pack, since hopefully they would only be staying a couple cycles. I hung back until they finished saying goodbye to the other members of their collective. They all looked worried. The collective was listed in the social feed as a group marriage, and had five children of various sizes. Once the others had left and Rami, Maro, and Tapan were alone, I came forward.

"Tlacey bought us passage on a public shuttle," Rami told me. "That could be a good sign, right?"

"Sure," I said. It was a terrible sign.

The employment voucher got me through into the embarkation zone and there was no weapons scan. Ravi-Hyral allowed private weapons and had a low security presence in public areas, which was one reason small groups of humans needed to hire private security consultants to go there. As we approached the shuttle's lock I sent to ART: *Can you scan the shuttle for energy anomalies without transit ring security detecting the activity?*

No, but I'll tell it I'm running scanning diagnostics and testing systems.

As we reached the lock, ART reported *No anomalies, 90 percent match to factory specs.*

That was normal, and meant if there was an explosive device, it was inert at the moment, buried somewhere inside the hull. Five other guest workers waited to board, and my scan read no energy signatures. They had stuffed packs and bags, indicating packing for a long-term stay. I let them board first, then slid in front of Maro and went through the lock, scanning as I went.

The shuttle was bot-driven and the only crew was one augmented human who seemed only there to check employment vouchers and shuttle passes. She looked at me and said, "There's only supposed to be three of you."

I didn't answer, being in the middle of wrestling the security system for control. It was an entirely separate system from the bot pilot, which was non-standard for the shuttles I was used to.

Tapan's chin jutted out. "This is our security consultant."

I had control of ShuttleSecSys, and deleted its attempt to alert the bot pilot and the crew member to the fact that it was compromised.

The crew member frowned, checked the voucher again, but didn't argue. We went on into the compartment where the other passengers were getting seated. They were stowing their possessions or talking quietly. I hadn't eliminated them as potential threats, but their behavior was lowering the probability at a steady rate.

I took a seat next to Rami as my clients got settled and pinged ART again. ART said, *I'm scanning for targeting anomalies and situation is currently clear.*

It meant it couldn't see anything on the moon aiming at us. If that was the plan, it wouldn't happen until we were underway. If somebody fired at the transit ring from the moon's surface, I was pretty sure that would be a huge deal and there would be legal ramifications, if not immediate violent retaliation by ring security. I told ART,

If they fire at us en route, it's not like we can do anything about it.

ART didn't answer, but I knew it well enough by now to know that meant something. I said, *You don't have a weapons system.* There hadn't been one on the schematics. At least the schematics that ART made available in its unsecured feed. *Do you?*

ART admitted, *I have a debris deflection system.*

There's only one way to deflect debris. I had never been on an armed ship but I knew they were subject to a whole different level of licensing and bond agreements. (If one of them accidentally shoots something it's not supposed to, somebody has to pay for the damage.) I said, *You have a weapons system.*

ART repeated, *For debris deflection.*

I was starting to wonder just what kind of university owned ART.

Rami was watching me worriedly. "Is everything okay?"

I nodded and tried to look neutral.

Tapan leaned past ter to ask, "Are you in the feed? I can't find you."

I told her, "I'm on a private channel with a friend in the ring who's monitoring the shuttle's departure. Just making sure everything's okay."

They nodded and sat back.

The shudder went through the deck that meant the shuttle had uncoupled from the ring and started to move. I cozied up to the bot pilot. It was a limited function model, not nearly as complex as even a standard transport driver bot. I had the ShuttleSecSys tell it I was authorized by ring security, and it pinged me cheerfully. The crew member was sitting in the cockpit with it, using her feed to catch up on admin tasks and read her social feed download, but there was no human pilot aboard.

I leaned back in my seat and relaxed a little. Media was tempting, and from the echoes I could pick up in the feed, that's what most of the humans were doing. But I wanted to keep monitoring the bot pilot. This may seem overcautious, but that's how I was built.

Then twenty-four minutes forty-seven seconds into the flight, as we were on approach, the bot pilot screamed and died as killware flooded its system. It was gone before ShuttleSecSys or I could react; I flung up a wall around us both and the killware bounced off. I saw it register task complete and then destroy itself.

Oh, shit. *ART!* I used ShuttleSecSys to grab the controls. We needed the course correction in seven point two seconds. The crew member, jolted out of her feed by the alarms, stared at the board in horror, then hit the emergency beacon. She couldn't fly a shuttle. I can fly hoppers and other upper atmosphere aircraft, but I had never been given the education module for shuttles or other space-going vehicles. I nudged ShuttleSecSys, hoping for help, and it set off all the cabin alarms. Yeah, that didn't help.

Let me in, ART said, as cool and calm as if we were discussing what show to watch next.

I had never given ART full access to my brain. I had let it alter my body, but not this. We had three seconds and counting. My clients, the other humans on the shuttle. I let it in.

It was like the sensation humans describe in books as having their heads shoved underwater. Then it was gone and ART was in the shuttle, using my connection with ShuttleSecSys to leap into the void left by the erased bot. ART flowed into the controls, made the course correction and adjusted our speed, then picked up the landing beacon and guided the shuttle into approach on the main RaviHyral port. The crew member had just managed to hail Port Authority, and was still hyperventilating. Port Authority had the ability to upload emergency landing routines, but the timing had been too tight. Nothing they could have done would have saved us.

Rami touched my arm and said, "Are you okay?"

I'd squeezed my eyes shut. "Yes," I told ter. Remembering that humans usually want more than that from other humans, I pointed up to indicate the alarms and added, "I've got sensitive hearing."

Rami nodded sympathetically. The others were worried, but there hadn't been an announcement and they could see our route in the feed from the port, which was still giving us an on-time arrival.

The crew member tried to explain to Port Authority that there had been a catastrophic failure, the pilot bot was gone, and she didn't know why the shuttle was following its normal route and not slamming into the surface of the moon. ShuttleSecSys tried to analyze ART and almost got itself deleted. I took over ShuttleSecSys, turned off the alarms, and deleted the entire trip out of its memory.

There were murmurs of relief from the passengers as the alarms stopped. I made a suggestion to ART, and it sent an error code to Port Authority, which assigned us a new priority and switched our landing site from the public dock to the emergency services dock. Since the killware had clearly been intended to destroy us en route, there might not be anybody waiting for us at our scheduled landing slot, but better safe than sorry.

The feed was giving us a visual of the port, which was inside a cavern, carved out of the side of a mountain, surrounded by the towers of a debris deflection grid. (An actual debris deflection system, as opposed to ART's concealed rail gun or whatever it had.) The lights of multiple levels of the port installation gleamed in the darkness, and smaller shuttles whizzed out of our way as we curved down toward the Port Authority's beacon.

Maro was watching me with narrowed eyes. When the notice of changed landing site came through the feed, she leaned forward and said, "You know what happened?"

Fortunately I remembered that nobody expected me to be compelled to answer all questions immediately. One of the benefits to being an augmented human security consultant rather than a construct SecUnit. I said, "We'll talk about it when we're off the shuttle," and they all seemed satisfied.

———

ART landed us in the Port Authority's slot. We left the shuttle crew member trying to explain to the emergency techs what had happened as they connected their diagnostic equipment. ART was already gone, deleting any evidence of its presence, and the ShuttleSecSys was confused, but at least still intact, unlike the poor pilot bot.

Emergency services personnel and bots milled around the small embarkation zone. I managed to herd my clients through and out onto the clear enclosed walkway to the main port before anyone thought to try to stop them. I had already downloaded a map from the public feed and was testing the robustness of the security system. The walkway had a view of the cavern, with the multiple levels of landing slots and a few shuttles coming and going. At the far end were the big haulers for the mining installations.

Security seemed to be intermittent and based on the level of paranoia of whatever contractor operated in the territory you were passing through. That could be both an advantage and an interesting challenge. The transit ring's public info feed had warned that a lot of humans apparently carried weapons here, and there were no screening scans.

We came out into a central hub, which had a high clear dome allowing a view of the cavern arching overhead, with lights trained on it to show off the colorful mineral veins. I scanned to make sure nothing was recording us and stopped Rami. Te and the others looked up at me and I said, "The person you're going to meet with just tried to kill you."

Rami blinked, Maro went wide-eyed, and Tapan drew breath to argue. I said, "The shuttle was infected with kill-ware. It destroyed the bot pilot. I was in contact with a friend who was able to use my augmented feed to download a new pilot module. That's the only reason we didn't crash."

A module could have put the shuttle into a safe orbit, but wouldn't have been sophisticated enough to manage the tricky, flawless landing. I was hoping they wouldn't realize that.

Tapan closed her mouth. Shocked, Maro said, "But the other passengers. The crew person. They would have killed everybody?"

I said, "If you were the only casualties, the motive would have been obvious."

I could see it was starting to sink in. I said, "You should return to the transit ring immediately." I checked the public feed for the schedule. There was a public shuttle leaving in eleven minutes. Tlacey wouldn't have time to trace my clients and infect it if they moved fast.

Tapan and Maro looked at Rami. Te hesitated, then set ter jaw and said, "I'll stay. You two go."

"No," Maro said instantly, "we're not leaving you." Tapan added, "We're in this together."

Rami's face almost crumpled, their support weakening ter when the prospect of death hadn't. Te controlled terself and nodded tightly. Te looked at me and said, "We'll stay."

I didn't react visibly, because I'm used to clients making bad decisions, and I was getting a lot of practice at controlling my expression. "You can't keep this meeting. They lost track of you when the shuttle didn't dock at its scheduled slot. You have to keep that advantage."

"But we have to have the meeting," Tapan protested. "We can't get our work back otherwise."

Yes, I often want to shake my clients. No, I never do. "Tlacey has no intention of giving you back your work. She lured you here to kill you."

"Yes, but—" Tapan began.

"Tapan, just hush and listen," Maro interrupted, clearly exasperated.

Rami looked stubborn, but asked, "Then what should we do?"

Technically, this didn't have to be my problem. I was here now and didn't need them anymore. I could lose them in the crowd and leave them to deal with their murderous ex-employer all on their own.

But they were clients. Even after I'd hacked my governor module, I'd found it impossible to abandon clients I hadn't chosen. I'd made an agreement with these clients as a free agent. I couldn't leave. I kept my sigh internal. "You can't meet Tlacey at her compound. You'll pick the spot."

It wasn't ideal, but it would have to do.

———

My clients picked a food service place in the center of the port. It was on a raised platform, the tables and chairs arranged in groups, with displays floating above advertising various port and contractor services and information about the different mining installations. The displays also functioned as camera and recording chaff, so the place was a popular spot for business meetings.

Rami, Tapan, and Maro had picked a table and were nervously fiddling with the drinks they had ordered from one of the bots drifting around. They had put in a comm call to Tlacey, and were waiting for a representative to arrive.

The security system in this public area was more sophisticated than ShuttleSecSys but not by much. I had gotten in far enough to monitor emergency traffic and get views from the cameras focused on our immediate area. I felt pretty confident. I was standing three meters from the table, pretending to look at the ad displays and examining the map of the installations I had found in the public feed. There were plenty of abandoned dig sites marked, as well as tube accesses that went off into apparently nowhere. Ganaka Pit had to be one of them.

ART said in my ear, *There must be an accessible information archive. Ganaka Pit's existence would not be deleted from it. The absence would be too obvious to researchers.*

That depended on the research. Someone working on strange synthetics would obviously care about where they were found, but not necessarily about what company had dug them up, or why that company wasn't around anymore. But whoever had removed Ganaka Pit from the map would have been trying to obscure its existence from casual journalists, not erase it entirely from the memory of the population.

ART's data had been correct; there were other SecUnits on this moon. The map showed logos from five bond companies that offered SecUnits, including my company, at seven of the most remote installations where exploration for mineral veins was still ongoing. They would be there to defend the claim from theft and to keep the miners and other employees from injuring each other as part of the bond guarantee. No SecUnits would travel through the port except as inert cargo in transport boxes or repair cubicles, so that was one less thing to worry about. My altered configuration might fool humans and augmented humans, but not other SecUnits.

If they saw me, they would alert their SecSystems. They wouldn't have a choice. And they wouldn't want one. If anybody knows how dangerous rogue SecUnits are, it's other SecUnits.

That was when I felt the ping.

I told myself I'd mistaken it for something else. Then it happened again. That's a big uh-oh.

Something was looking for SecUnits. Not just bots, specifically SecUnits, and it was close. It hadn't pinged me directly, though if I'd had a working governor module, I would have been compelled to answer.

Three humans approached the table my clients were sitting at. Rami whispered into ter feed, "That's Tlacey. I didn't expect her to come herself." Two of the humans were large and male and one of them lengthened his stride to reach the table. Maro had seen him and from the look on her face I knew this was not going to be a greeting. Scan showed he was armed.

I moved between him and the table. I put a hand up at his chest height and said, "Stop."

On most contracts this was as far as I was allowed to go with a human until they made physical contact. But you'd be surprised how often this works, if you do it right. Though that was when I was wearing my armor with the helmet opaqued. Standing here in normal human clothes with my human face showing made it a whole different thing. But it wasn't like he could hurt me by hitting me and he hadn't drawn his weapon yet.

I could have torn through him like tissue paper.

He didn't know that, but he must have been able to tell from my face that I wasn't afraid of him. I checked the security camera to see what I looked like, and decided I looked bored. That wasn't unusual, because I almost always looked bored while I was doing my job, it was just impossible to tell when I was in my armor.

He visibly regrouped and said, "Who the fuck are you?"

My clients had shoved their chairs back and were on their feet. Rami said, "This is our security consultant."

He stepped back, and glanced uncertainly at the other two, the second male human bodyguard and Tlacey, who was an augmented human female.

I dropped my arm but didn't move. I had clear shots at all three of them, but that was a worst-case scenario. For me, at least. Humans can miss a lot of little clues, but me being able to fire energy weapons from my arms would be something of a red flag. I diverted just enough attention to scan the security camera feeds for whatever it was that had pinged me.

I caught an image on a camera across the public area, near one of the entrance tunnels. The figure standing near the edge of the seating area didn't match what I was expecting to see and I had to review it again before I understood. It wasn't wearing armor and its physical configuration didn't match SecUnit standard. It had a lot of hair, silver with blue and purple on the ends, pulled back and braided like Tapan's but in a much more complicated pattern. Its facial features were different from mine, but all Units' features are different, assigned randomly based on the human cloned material that's used to make our organic parts. Its arms were bare, and there was no metal showing and no gun ports. This was not a SecUnit.

I was looking at a sexbot.

That is not the official designation, ART said.

The official designation is ComfortUnit but everybody knows what that means.

Sexbots aren't allowed to walk around in human areas without orders, any more than murderbots. Someone must have sent it here.

ART poked me hard enough to make me twitch. I snapped out of it and ran my recording back a little to catch up on what was happening.

Tlacey had stepped forward. "And just why do you need a security consultant?"

Rami took a breath. I hit ter feed, secured a private connection between ter, Tapan, and Maro, and told ter, *Don't answer that. Don't mention the attempt on the shuttle. Just stick to business.* It was an impulse. Tlacey had come here expecting an angry confrontation; that was why she had brought armed bodyguards. We had an advantage now; we weren't dead, and they were off balance and we wanted to keep them that way.

Rami let the breath out, tapped my feed in acknowledgment, then said, "We're here to talk about our files."

Maro, who had realized what I was trying to do, told Rami, *Keep going, don't even let them sit down.*

Sounding more confident, Rami continued, "Deleting our personal work was not part of our employment contract. But we'll agree to your proposal that we return our signing bonus in exchange for our files."

On the security cameras, I watched the sexbot turn and leave the public area via the tunnel directly behind it.

Tlacey said, "The entire bonus?" She clearly hadn't expected them to agree.

Maro leaned forward. "We opened an account with Umro to hold the funds. We can transfer it to you as soon as you give us the files."

Tlacey's jaw moved as she spoke in her private feed. The two bodyguards eased back. Tlacey stepped over and took a chair at my clients' table. After a moment, Rami sat down, and Tapan and Maro followed suit.

I kept part of my attention on the negotiation, and went back to the public feed. I started pulling historical data, looking for any irregular activity around the time of my contract here.

While my clients were talking, and while I sorted through the data with ART peering over my shoulder again, I was watching the security cameras. I noted two more potential threats enter the area. Both were augmented humans. I had noted three potential threats already sitting at adjacent tables. (All three exhibited a

curious lack of attention toward the confrontation occurring near the center of the seating area. The other humans
and augmented humans in the immediate area had
watched it with open or surreptitious curiosity.)

ART poked me. *I see it,* I told it. The search had turned
up a series of notices posted around the right timeframe.
They were warnings that changes in shipments of raw materials and supplies to outlying installations would cause
diversions in the passenger tube routes. (The tube was a
small-scale transit system that took passengers around
the port and service centers and had private lines going
out to the closer mining installations.) Later notices mentioned a new route that had been constructed to compensate for the diversion.

That was it. Reading between the lines, you could see
that the service contractors had had to build a new tube
route to bypass the tunnels that had led to a mining installation that had abruptly closed. That had to be the site
of Ganaka Pit.

Other pit closures had been accompanied by local interest articles and excessive social feed interest in bank-
ruptcy filings and the effect on the associated service
companies. There was nothing like that about this clo-
sure. Someone had paid to have those postings deleted
from the public feed.

The conversation was concluding. Tlacey stood up,

nodded to my clients, and walked away from the table. Rami's expression was a grimace of doubt. Maro looked grim and Tapan somewhere between confused and angry.

I closed the search and stepped over to the table. Watching Tlacey and her bodyguards leave, Rami said, "It was a bad idea to come here."

Tapan protested, "She said tomorrow . . ."

Maro shook her head. "It's more lies. She isn't going to give us the files. She could have done it here, if she was going to do it. She could have done it over the comm while we were on the transit ring." She looked up at me. "I wasn't sure I believed you about the shuttle, but now . . ."

I was keeping track of my potential threat list on the security cameras. "We need to go," I told them. "We'll talk about this somewhere else."

As we left, one potential threat got up to follow us. I tapped ART to keep an eye on the others, just in case they weren't innocent bystanders so deep in their feeds they really hadn't noticed anything.

I had marked a few possible routes on the station map, and my favorite one was through a pedestrian tunnel that curved out away from the main living areas. There were various accesses along it leading to different tube stations, but it was not a popular route. I tapped Rami's feed and told ter to take it toward the interchange where the largest hotel was. Listening in, Maro whispered, "We can't afford that one."

You won't be staying there, I told them on the feed. The brochure on the public feed promised a high security lobby area and a fast tube access to the public shuttle slots.

We reached the tunnel and started down it. It was close to ten meters wide and four meters high, well-lit enough for walking down the center, but the sides were shadowy with darkened branching tunnels. There were security cameras, but the system monitoring them was not sophisticated. The company would have shit itself over the possible danger to bonded clients and the missed opportunity to data mine conversations.

There were other humans in the tunnel. Some miners in coveralls and jackets with logos from the various installations, but most were in civilian work clothes, either techs or workers for the support companies. They moved quickly and stayed in groups.

After eight minutes of walking, most of the other humans in the tunnel had turned off to one of the tube access points. I sent through the feed, *Just keep walking, don't stop. I'll meet you in the lobby.* I dropped back into one of the darker branching tunnels. My clients kept moving and didn't look back at me, though I could tell Tapan wanted to.

On the cameras I watched Potential Threat/New Target

make his way up the tunnel, walking quickly. He was joined by two new humans, now designated Target Two and Target Three. They passed me and I came out of the tube access and followed at a distance. I scanned them for energy weapons and found no readings. All three Targets wore jackets and pants with deep side pockets. I marked seven locations where knives or extendable batons could be carried.

When they caught sight of my clients, the Targets slowed down but continued to reduce the distance between them. I knew they were probably reporting to someone on their feed, asking for instructions. Whoever it was didn't have control of the security cameras, at least not yet.

I followed, watching the targets through my eyes, through the security cameras, watching myself to make sure I wasn't drawing attention, that no one was following me. ART kept quiet, though I could tell it was interested in watching me work.

Then the last group of miners between me and the Targets turned into a tube access. We were in a bend of the tunnel and there was no one between my clients and the next bend some fifty meters ahead, and the security cameras showed me the tunnel was empty behind me. I needed to get this over with. I turned into the tube access behind the miners.

I stopped at the top of the tube access while the miners boarded the capsule. The door hissed as it closed and the capsule moved away. On security camera view, Target Two's jaw moved, indicating that he was speaking subvocally in his feed. Then the camera's feed cut off.

I turned the corner back into the tunnel and started to run.

It was a calculated risk, as I couldn't move at top speed without revealing I wasn't human. But I managed to arrive just as Target One reached Rami and grabbed the sleeve of ter jacket. I broke his arm and slammed an elbow into his chin, then swung him into Target Two, who had turned toward me with the knife he had been approaching Maro with. Target Two accidentally (I'm guessing here; maybe they just didn't care for each other) stabbed Target One. Target Two staggered sideways and I dropped Target One, and broke Target Two's kneecap. Target Three had had time to lift his baton and now hit me across the left side of my head and shoulder which, granted, annoyed me a little, but I've had hauler bots hit me harder than that by accident. I blocked the second blow with my left arm, snapped his collarbone with one punch, and smashed his hip with another.

He was lucky I wasn't a lot annoyed.

All three Targets were on the floor, and Two was the

only one who was still conscious, though he was curled up and whimpering. I turned to my clients.

Rami had a hand over ter mouth, Maro was frozen in place, staring, and Tapan had thrown her hands up in the air. I said in the feed, *Go to the hotel, wait for me in the lobby. Don't run, walk.*

Maro came out of shock first. She nodded hard, caught Rami's arm, and poked Tapan's shoulder. Rami turned to go, but Tapan said, "Security?"

I knew what she was asking. "They told somebody to cut the cameras. That's why you need to leave now." The public feed up on the transit ring had said there was no overall security, but the security companies for the different service installations and contractors were supposed to take responsibility for the public areas nearest their territory. This spot had obviously been carefully calculated to be out of range of any immediate assistance by whoever had helped the Targets by cutting the camera feed. I wasn't expecting an immediate response, but we did need to move relatively quickly.

Rami whispered, "Come on," and they started away, walking fast but not running.

I turned to the Target that was still conscious and pressed down on the artery in his neck until he passed out.

I started away, walking at a normal pace. I was deep enough into the camera system to delete the temporary storage on the cameras ahead of and behind the deactivated camera. That would help obscure the issue for anybody trying to figure out what had happened. But Tlacey had seen me, and she would know. I was just hoping the kids listened to me this time.

———————

I reached the interchange where various access tunnels and tube stations met, with a scatter of pop-up stands selling packaged food, feed interfaces, toiletries, and other things humans liked. It wasn't crowded but there was a steady flow of foot traffic. The hotel entrance was on the far side.

The lobby was built on various platforms overlooking a holo sculpture of an open chasm filled with a giant crystalline structure growing out of the walls. From the notations in the feed, it was supposed to be educational, but I had serious doubts about whether the mines on Ravi-Hyral looked like that. Especially after the mining bots got to them.

My clients were on the same platform as the check-in area, near the railing around the sculpture's artificial chasm, sitting on a round backless couch thing that looked more like a decorative object than furniture.

I sat on my heels in front of them.

Rami said, "They were going to kill us."

"Again," I said.

Rami bit ter lip. "I believed you about the shuttle. I believed you . . ."

"But now you've seen it," I said. I knew what te meant. There was a huge difference between knowing something happened and seeing the reality of it. Even for SecUnits.

Maro rubbed her eyes. "Yeah, we were idiots. Tlacey was never going to let us give her the bonus for our files."

"No, she wasn't," I agreed.

Rami nudged her. "You were right."

Maro looked more depressed. "I didn't want to be."

Tapan said miserably, "We're wrecked."

Rami put an arm around her. "We're alive." Te looked at me. "What do we do now?"

I said, "Let me get you out of here."

Chapter Six

I TOOK THEM TO the public shuttle slots first, then past that section to the private docks. Checking the schedules, ART had already scanned a likely shuttle. It was privately owned but the frequency of its trips to and from the transit ring suggested an entrepreneur who was offering private rides for hard currency.

This proved to be accurate, and it would allow Rami, Maro, and Tapan to leave without their employment vouchers being scanned. It would probably have been safe at this point to put them on a public shuttle, as long as there was no advance notice of which one they were taking. Killware couldn't travel over the feed to infect a shuttle; there were too many protections in place. Whoever had planned to kill us on arrival had had to deliver the killware directly, through a data port actually inside the shuttle's cockpit.

But I'm programmed to be paranoid. This private shuttle had the benefit not only of anonymity, but of an augmented human pilot who would be in place in case something interfered with the bot pilot. Plus ART, who was already cozying up to said bot pilot and would be keeping an eye on the shuttle during the brief trip. (ART's idea of "cozying" being somewhat overbearing, I had already had to intervene once to assure the bot pilot that the big mean transport had promised not to hurt it.)

"You're not going with us?" Rami asked, standing in the small embarkation area. The private docks were dingy and small compared to the Port Authority's docks, with stains on the metal partitions and some of the lights up in the rocky ceiling broken or dim. Humans and a few bots were moving along the walkway above us, and I kept an eye on both approaches through the security cameras. The shuttle was already loaded into its slot and its hatch was open, with a small augmented human standing on the ramp to take the money. Six other passengers had already boarded and it was taking a large portion of my self-control not to just scoop up my clients and carry them onboard.

I said, "I still need to do some research here. I'll go back to the transit ring when I'm finished."

"How do we pay you?" Maro asked. "I mean, can we still afford you after . . . everything?" *After they tried to kill us,* she added in our joint feed connection.

"I'll check my social feed profile on the ring," I said, and felt pretty good that I had even remembered it existed. "Send a note to me there, and I'll find you when I get back."

"It's just, I know we're—" Tapan glanced around. Her expression was tense and unhappy, her body language bordering on desperate. "We can't stay here, but I can't give up, either. Our work—"

I said, "Sometimes people do things to you that you can't do anything about. You just have to survive it and go on."

They all stopped talking and stared at me. It made me nervous and I immediately switched my view to the nearest security camera so I could watch us from the side. I had said it with more emphasis than I intended, but it was just the way things were. I wasn't sure why it had such an impact on them. Maybe I sounded like I knew what I was talking about. Maybe it was the two murder attempts.

Then Maro nodded, her mouth set in a grim line. She and Rami looked at each other and Rami nodded sadly. Maro said, "We need to get back to the others, figure out what to do next. Look for the next assignment."

Rami added, "We'll start over. We did it once, we can do it again."

Tapan looked like she wanted to protest, but was too depressed to argue.

They wanted to say goodbye a lot and thank me, and I herded them up to the ramp while they were doing it, and watched Rami pay for their passage with a currency card that the crew person pressed to an interface. Then they were aboard.

The hatch closed and the shuttle's feed signaled post-boarding mode, waiting for its clearance to leave. I went back down the access, heading for the walkway. I needed to get the tube over to the area where the tunnel diversion had occurred and start searching for Ganaka Pit. It was a relief to have my clients headed back to safety. But it felt odd to be on my own again, working for no one except myself.

I went to the tube access and boarded the next capsule to stop. Each capsule had seating for twenty people, plus an overhead rack to hold on to. The gravity was adjusted inside the cab to compensate for the motion. I took a seat with the seven humans already aboard. ART said, *The shuttle has launched. I'll monitor your feed, but much of my attention will be on it.*

I sent an acknowledgment. I was trying to isolate why I felt so uneasy. Trapped in a small enclosed space with humans, check. Missing my drones, check. My Giant Asshole Research Transport too busy to complain at, check. Needed to actually focus on what I was doing so couldn't watch media, check. But that wasn't what it was. I hadn't done a good job for my clients. I had had the opportunity, and had failed. As a SecUnit, I had the responsibility for my clients' safety but no authority to do anything other than make suggestions, and try to use the company regulations inbuilt in a SecSystem to override the humans' suicidal stupidity and homicidal impulses. This time I had responsibility and authority, and had still failed.

I told myself they were alive, I just hadn't gotten their property back, which had actually not been part of the job they hired me for. It didn't help.

I got off the tube on the far end of its circuit. This was a warren of tunnels that according to the map led off to various private tube accesses for the distant mining pits. Only a few humans got off the tube here, all heading immediately down the tunnel for the nearest tube interchange. I went the other direction.

I spent the next hour hacking cameras and security barriers, slipping in and out of half-completed tunnels, many with warning markers for air quality. Finally I located one that showed evidence of past use as a mining access. It was big enough for the largest hauler bots, and the cameras and lights were down. As I went along it, climbing over rock and metal debris, I felt the public feed drop out.

I stopped and checked ART's comm, but it was only picking up static. I didn't think it was any deliberate attempt to block my connection to the rest of the installation; I'd experienced that type of outage before and this felt different. I think this tunnel was so deep below the surface that the comm and the feed needed powered relays to get out, and those weren't functioning anymore. Something ahead still had power, because my feed was picking up intermittent signals, all automated warnings. I kept going.

I had to open another security barrier, but past it found a cargo tube access and managed to push the sliding door open. A small passenger tube was still there. It hadn't been used in a long time, long enough for the water and scattered trash on the carpet to combine and grow something squishy. I made my way up to the front compartment where the manual emergency controls were. There was still power in the batteries, though not much. It had been left here, forgotten, slowly dying in the darkness as the hours ticked away.

Not that I was feeling morbid, or anything.

I checked to make sure there was no active security attached to it, then got it started. It groaned into life, lifted off the ground, and started down the tunnel into darkness, following its last programmed route. I sat down on the bench to wait.

Finally the tube's scan picked up a blockage ahead and threw an alarm code. I had five episodes of different drama series, two comedies, a book about the history of the exploration of alien remnants in the Corporation Rim, and a multi-part art competition from Belal Tertiary Eleven queued and paused, but I was actually watching episode 206 of *Sanctuary Moon*, which I'd already seen twenty-seven times. Yes, I was a little nervous. When the tube started to slow, I sat up.

The lights shone on a line of metal barricades. Glowing markers had been sprayed on the material, sending out bursts of warning into my feed. Radiation hazard, falling rock hazard, toxic biological hazard. I got the emergency lock to unseal for me and jumped down to the gritty ground. I was scanning for energy signatures and I adjusted my eyesight to be able to see past the bright marker paint. There was a gap three meters along, a darker patch against the metal. It was small but I didn't have to pop any joints to wriggle through.

I walked down the tunnel to the platform that had been part of the passenger tube access. Farther down there was a set of ten-meter-high doors, big enough for vehicles and the largest hauler bots to maneuver through and for the loads of raw mineral to come out. The passenger access had a cargo unloading rack still extended, and I used it to swing up to the high platform. Everything was covered with a layer of damp dust, which showed no recent tracks. The sealed crates of a supply delivery, with the logos of various contractors stamped on the boxes, still stood stacked on the platform. A broken breather mask lay beside it. My human parts were experiencing a cold prickling that wasn't comfortable. This place was creepy. I reminded myself that the terrible thing that had most likely happened here was me.

Somehow that didn't help.

There wasn't enough power to move the doors, but the manual release for the passenger access lock still worked. There was no powered light in the corridor either, but the walls were streaked with light-emitting markers, meant to guide everyone out in the event of a catastrophic failure. Some had already failed with age, others were fading. The lack of any feed activity except from the warning paint was vaguely disturbing; I kept thinking of the Delt-Fall habitat and I was glad I had had ART make the adjustment to my data port.

I followed the corridor into the installation's central hub. It was a large domed area, dark except for the fading markers on the ground. There were no human remains, of course, but debris was scattered around, tools, broken slivers of plastic, a chunk of hauler bot arm. Openings to corridors, like dark caves, branched off in all directions. I had no sense of having been here before, no sense of familiarity. I identified the passages that led toward the mine pit, then the corridors that went toward the quarters and offices. Branching off from that was the equipment storage.

The emergency power failure releases for the sealed doors had unlocked everything, but whoever had cleaned up afterward had left them shut, and I had to shove each one open. Past the maintenance stations for the hauler bots, I found the security ready room. I stepped in and froze. In the dimness, among the empty weapon storage boxes and the missing floor panels where the recycler had stood, there were familiar shapes. The cubicles were still here.

There were ten of them lined up against the far wall, big smooth white boxes, the dim marker light gleaming off the scuffed surfaces. I didn't know why my performance reliability was dropping, why it was so hard to move. Then I realized it was because I thought the others were still in there.

It was a completely irrational thought that would have confirmed ART's bad opinion of the mental abilities of constructs. They wouldn't leave SecUnits here. We were too expensive, too dangerous to abandon. If I wasn't locked inside one of these cubicles, the organic part of my brain dreaming, the rest helpless and inert, then the others weren't here.

It was still hard to make myself cross the room and open the first door.

The plastic bed inside was empty, the power long cut off. I opened each one, but it was the same.

I stepped back from the last one. I wanted to bury my face in my hands, sink down to the floor, and slip into my media, but I didn't. After twelve long seconds, the intense feeling subsided.

I don't even know why I'd come in here. I needed to look for data storage, records left behind. I checked the weapons lockers to make sure there was nothing handy, like a package of drones, but they were empty. A firefight had left burn scars on the wall and there was a small crater impact from an explosive projectile next to one of the cubicles. Then I went back toward the offices.

I found the installation control center. Broken display surfaces were everywhere, chairs overturned, interfaces shattered on the floor, and a plastic cup still sat on a console, undisturbed, waiting for someone to pick it up again. Humans can't work completely in the feed with multiple inputs the way I can, and bots like ART can. Some augmented humans have implanted interfaces that allow it, but not all humans want lots of things inserted into their brains, go figure. So they need these surfaces to project displays for group work. And the external data storage should be tied in here somewhere.

I picked a station, set a chair upright, and got out the small toolkit I had borrowed from ART's crew storage and brought along in the large side pocket of my pants. (Armor doesn't have pockets, so score one for ordinary human clothing.) I needed a power source to get the station operable again, but fortunately I had me.

I used the tools to open a port on the energy weapon in my right forearm. Doing it one-handed was tricky, but I've had to do worse. I used a patch cord to connect me to the console's emergency power access and then the station hummed as it powered up. I couldn't open the feed to control it directly, but I reached into the glittering projection and fished out the access for the Security Systems recorded storage. It had been wiped, but I'd been expecting that.

I started to check all the other storage, just in case it hadn't been the company techs who had wiped SecSystem. The company wants everything recorded, work done in the feed, conversations, everything, so they can data mine it. A lot of that information is useless and gets deleted, but SecSystem has to hold on to it until the data mining bots can go over it, and so SecSystem often steals unused temporary storage space from other systems.

And there they were, files tucked into the MedSystem's storage space for non-standard procedure downloads. (Presumably if MedSystem suddenly needed to download an emergency procedure for a patient, SecSystem would have whisked the files out and put them somewhere else, but sometimes it couldn't act in time and chunks of recorded data would be lost. If you're a SecUnit and you like your clients and want to keep something they've said or done (or that you've said or done) away from the company, this is one of the many ways you can make files accidentally disappear.)

SecSystem must have shifted files over right before the power failure. There was a lot of material and I skipped past random conversations and mining operations data to the end, then scrolled back a little. In the feed, two human techs had discussed an anomaly, some code that didn't seem to be associated with any system, that had been uploaded on-site. They were trying to figure out where it had come from, and speculating, with a lot of profanity, that the installation had been bombed with malware. One tech said she was going to notify the supervisor, that they needed to sequester SecSystem, and the conversation ended there, in mid-word.

That was . . . not what I was expecting. I'd assumed a malfunction of my governor module had caused the massacre the company euphemistically referred to as an "incident." But had I really taken out nine other Sec-Units, plus all the bots and any armed humans who might have tried to stop me? I didn't like my chances. If the other SecUnits had experienced the same malfunction, it had to come from an outside source.

I saved the conversation to my own storage, checked the other systems for stray files but found nothing, and unhooked myself from the console.

The security ready room had been stripped to the bone. But there were other places I could check. I pushed away from the console.

As I went through the other door, I noticed the impact points in the wall opposite, the stains on the floor. Someone—something capable of taking a high degree of injury had made a last stand here, trying to defend the control center. Maybe not all the SecUnits had been affected.

In the corridor near the living quarters, I found the other ready room, the one for the ComfortUnits.

Inside were four shapes that were clearly cubicles, but smaller. Their doors stood open, the plastic beds inside empty. In the corner there was space for a recycler, but no weapons lockers, and the storage cabinets were all different.

I stood in the center of the room. The cubicles for the murderbots had been closed, not in use. Which meant none of the SecUnits had been damaged and all had been either out on patrol, on guard, or in the ready room, probably standing around pretending not to stare at each other. But the cubicles for the sexbots were open, which meant they had been inside when the emergency occurred and the power shut off. If the power is off, you can manually open a cubicle from the inside, but it won't shut again.

It meant they had deployed during the "incident."

I used the energy weapon in my arm again to power the first cubicle's emergency data storage. I didn't have anywhere near the energy needed to get the whole thing powered up, but the data storage box is for holding error and shutdown information if something goes wrong during a repair. (There are a lot of other things you can do with it if you've hacked your governor module, like use it to temporarily store your media so the human techs won't find it.) SecSystem might have used it before its catastrophic failure.

It had been used. But by the ComfortUnits, to download their data during the incident.

It was patchy and hard to put together, until I realized the ComfortUnits had been communicating with each other.

I stood there for five hours and twenty-three minutes, putting the data fragments together.

There had been a code download from another mining installation for the ComfortUnits, supposedly a patch purchased from a third party ComfortUnit supplier. The ComfortUnits had all flagged it as non-standard and needing review by SecSystem and the human systems analyst, but the techs who had downloaded it ordered them to apply it. It turned out to be well-disguised malware. It hadn't affected the ComfortUnits, but had used their feeds to jump to SecSystem and infect it. SecSystem had infected the SecUnits, bots, and drones, and everything capable of independent motion in the installation had lost its mind.

In between the running and shooting and the humans screaming in the background, the ComfortUnits had managed to analyze the malware and discover it was supposed to jump from them to the hauler bots and shut them down. This would disrupt operations so the other mining installation could get their shipment to the cargo transport first. This had been a sabotage attempt, not a mass murder. But a mass murder was what was happening.

The humans had managed to get an alert out to the port, but it was clear help would not arrive in time. The ComfortUnits noted that the SecUnits were not acting in concert, and were also attacking each other, while the bots randomly smashed into anything that moved. The ComfortUnits had decided that taking SecSystem back to factory default via its manual interface was their best option.

ComfortUnits are more physically powerful than a human, but not a SecUnit or bot. They had no inbuilt weapons, and while they could pick up a projectile or energy weapon and use it, they had no education modules on how the weapons worked. They could pick one up, try to aim it, pull the trigger, and hope the safety wasn't engaged.

One by one the file downloads had stopped. One had signaled that it would try to decoy SecUnit attention away from the others, and three acknowledged. One had heard screams from the control center and diverted there to try to save the humans trapped inside, and two acknowledged. One had stayed at the entrance to a corridor to try to buy time to reach SecSystem, and one acknowledged. One reported reaching SecSystem, then nothing.

I caught a low power warning from my own system and realized how long I had been here. I unhooked myself from the cubicle and left the room. I bumped into the edge of the doorway and the wall.

There must have been some off-the-books arrangement, maybe the installation who supplied the malware paid for the damages and the bonds, which might have been such a large amount that the installation had then failed and ceased operation. Maybe the company thought that was punishment enough.

I made my way back to the tube, climbed inside, and

started a recharge cycle. Once I had enough capacity, I went back to episode 206 of *Sanctuary Moon*.

———————

The tube ran out of power and died short of the access, but fortunately I was back up to 97 percent capacity by that time. I got out and ran the rest of the way. Running isn't tiring for me the way it is for a human, but I reached the sealed access fifty-eight minutes later than I would have on the tube.

It had been a long, shitty cycle, and I was ready for it to be over with. I wanted to get off this mine only slightly less than I had probably wanted to get off it the first time I was here.

I had gotten back through the security barrier and was walking up the tunnel when I came within range of the feed again. I tapped ART to let it know I was back.

It said, *We have a problem.*

Chapter Seven

I LOCATED THE PROBLEM in the lobby of the main hotel.

Tapan was on one of the upper platforms, seated on a round cushioned bench, her pack at her feet, partially screened by another holographic sculpture of a giant crystal formation. She looked up at me and said, "Oh, hi. I didn't know if the others would be able to reach you."

Without me present in the shuttle, ART hadn't had any visual access to the passenger compartment. (As a private vehicle that was only being used as a public transport in a sketchy if not openly illegal way, it had no onboard security system or cameras.) ART hadn't known Tapan wasn't onboard until the shuttle reached the transit ring. Taking its responsibility seriously, it had sent a drone over to the embarkation area to watch my clients disembark and had seen an obviously distraught and angry Rami and Maro, but no Tapan. Then it had checked Eden's profile on the social media feed and found the message from Rami. (Tapan had told them she was sick and was going to the shuttle's restroom compartment. They hadn't realized what had happened until the shuttle had cleared the port.)

I said, "They left me a message." I had intended to just stand there and stare at her, which is what SecUnits do to clients who have just performed an act of stupidity so profound it approaches suicide which they ordered us not to stop them from doing. But she looked like she knew she had been stupid, and I had to know. "What happened?"

She looked up at me, clearly anticipating a negative reaction. "I got a note in my feed, through the social profile I had when we were working here. Someone working for Tlacey—a friend—said he had copies of the files and he'd give them to us." She forwarded the message to my feed.

I checked it carefully. The meeting time was set for the next cycle.

I felt this would be the point where a human would sigh, so I sighed.

Tapan said, "I know it could be a trap, but, maybe it isn't? I know him, he's not the greatest guy, but he hates Tlacey." She hesitated. "Will you help me? Please? I'll understand if you say no. I know I've been . . . I know this could be a really bad idea."

I had forgotten that I had a choice, that I wasn't obligated to do what she wanted just because she was here.

Being asked to stay, with a please and an option for refusal, hit me almost as hard as a human asking for my opinion and actually listening to me. I sighed again. I was having a lot of opportunities to do it and I think I was getting good at it. "I'll help you. Right now we need to find a place to get out of sight."

———————

Tapan had a hard currency card from the transit ring, which wasn't tied to any RaviHyral account and so was not traceable. At least, that's what she thought and I hoped she was right. I had never been given any education modules on financial systems and since our modules were crap anyway, I'm not sure that would have helped. ART ran a search for me and the results were mixed. Hard currency cards could be traced, but usually only by noncorporate political or corporate entities. I decided it was probably all right to use it. If the message wasn't a trap, Tlacey must think my clients were back on the transit ring by now. If it was a trap, they would know they could grab us when we walked into the meeting so there was no point in looking for us earlier.

Tapan used the card to pay for a transient room in the block next to the port. While she ran the card through the vending kiosk and got our room assignment, I stood behind her and surveyed the area. The transient rooms were in a narrow warren of corridors, as unlike the main hotel as a real cargo transport was unlike ART. There was no SecSystem to get control of and only one camera at the entrance. I deleted us out of its memory, but I still felt like we—or I—might have been observed at some point. It might just be inherent rogue-SecUnit-on-the-run paranoia.

Tapan led the way to our room. There were other humans hanging around the dimly lit corridors and some looked like they might try to approach her, then saw me and changed their minds. I was bigger than they were, and without cameras it was still hard to control my expression.

ART said, *Tell the human not to touch any surfaces. There may be disease vectors present.*

On the way here I had shared the recording of what I had found at Ganaka Pit. ART said, *This is good news. You were not at fault.* I agreed, sort of. I had been expecting to feel better about it. I mostly just felt awful.

Once inside the room with the door secured, I saw Tapan's shoulders relax and she took a deep breath. The room was just a square box with pads stored in a cabinet for sitting or sleeping, and a small display surface. No cameras, no audio surveillance. There was a tiny attached bath, with a waste-reclaimer and a shower. At least it had a door. I was going to have to pretend to use it at least twice. Yes, that would be the cap on all the fun I was having today. I created a schedule and set an alarm to remind myself to do it.

Tapan dropped her bag on the floor and faced me. "I know you're mad."

I tried to moderate my expression. "I'm not mad." I was furious. I thought my clients were safe, I was free to worry about my own problems, and now I had a tiny human to look after that I couldn't possibly abandon.

She nodded and pushed her braids back. "I know—I mean—I'm sure Rami and Maro were furious. But it's not like I'm not afraid, so that's good."

In my feed, ART said, *What?*

I have no idea, I told it. I said to Tapan, "How is that good?"

She explained, "In the creche, our moms always said that fear was an artificial condition. It's imposed from the outside. So it's possible to fight it. You should do the things you're afraid of."

If a bot with a brain the size of a transport could roll its eyes, that was what ART was doing. I said, "That isn't the purpose of fear." They didn't give us an education module on human evolution, but I had looked it up in the

HubSystem knowledge bases I'd had access to, in an effort to figure out what the hell was going on with humans. It hadn't helped.

She said, "I know, it's supposed to be inspirational." She looked around and went to the cabinet with the seating pads. She pulled them out, sniffed them suspiciously, then took an aerosol capsule out of a pocket on her pack and sprayed them down. "I forgot to ask, did you get a chance to do the research you wanted to do here?"

"Yes. It was . . . inconclusive." It had been damningly conclusive, it just hadn't had the revelatory effect I had been, stupidly, hoping for. I helped her pull the rest of the pads out.

We got them arranged on the floor and sat down. She looked at me and bit her lip. "You're really augmented, aren't you. Like, a lot. Like more than someone would choose voluntarily."

It wasn't a question. I said, "Um, yes."

She nodded. "Was it an accident?"

I realized I had my arms wrapped around myself and was leaning over like I was trying to go into a fetal position. I don't know why this was so stressful. Tapan wasn't afraid of me. I had no reason to be afraid of her. Maybe it was being here again, seeing Ganaka Pit again. Some part of my organic systems remembered what had happened there. In the feed, ART started to play the soundtrack to *Sanctuary Moon* and weirdly, that helped. I said, "I got caught in an explosion. There's not much of me that's human, actually."

Both those statements are true.

She stirred a little, as if debating what to say, then nodded again. "I'm sorry I got you into this. I know you know what you're doing, but . . . I have to try, I have to see if this guy really has our files. Just this once, and then I'll go back to the transit ring."

In my feed, ART turned down the soundtrack to say, *Young humans can be impulsive. The trick is keeping them around long enough to become old humans. This is what my crew tells me and my own observations seem to confirm it.*

I couldn't argue with the wisdom dispensed by ART's absent crew. I remembered humans had needs and asked Tapan, "Did you eat?"

She had bought some meal packs with the hard currency card and had them stuffed in her bag. She offered me one and I told her my augments required me to have a special diet and it wasn't time for me to eat yet. She accepted that readily. Humans apparently don't like to discuss catastrophic injuries to digestive systems, so I didn't need any of the corroborating detail ART had just researched for me. I asked her if she liked media and she said yes, so I sent some files to the display surface in the room, and we watched the first three episodes of *World-hoppers*. ART was pleased, and I could feel it sitting in my feed, comparing Tapan's reactions to the show to mine.

When Tapan said she wanted to try to sleep, I shut down the display. She curled up on her pad and I lay down on mine and continued watching in the feed with ART.

Two hours and forty-three minutes later, I caught a ping from right outside the door.

I sat up so abruptly, Tapan woke with a start. I motioned for her to be quiet, and she subsided back on the pad, curling around her pack, looking worried. I stood and went to the door, listening. I couldn't hear any breathing, but there was a change in the background noise that told me there was something solid on the other side of the metal door. Cautiously, I did a limited scan.

Yes, there was something out there, but no sign of weapons. I checked the ping and saw it had the same signature as the ping I had caught in the public area during the meeting with Tlacey.

The sexbot was standing on the other side of the door.

It couldn't have been following me all this time. It could have been watching for me on the security cameras, tracking me sporadically through the port when I came back within range. That was not a comforting thought.

It had to belong to Tlacey. If it had been watching me, it would have missed Tapan's unexpected exit from the private shuttle but would have seen her again when we met up at the main hotel or on the way here. Damn it.

But now I knew that. If it hadn't pinged me, I wouldn't have realized it was in play. *Why is it here?* I asked ART.

I assume that's a rhetorical question, it said.

There was only one way to find out. I acknowledged the ping.

The moment stretched. Then it reached out to my feed. It was cautious, the connection almost tentative. It said, *I know what you are. Who sent you?*

I replied, *I'm on contract to a private individual. Why are you communicating with me?*

SecUnits on the same contract don't talk, either verbally or on the feed, unless they absolutely have to in order to perform their duties. Communicating with units on different contracts has to be done through the controlling HubSystems. And SecUnits don't interact with ComfortUnits anyway. Could this be a rogue sexbot? If it was rogue, why was it here on RaviHyral? I didn't know why anybody would stay here voluntarily, including the humans. No, it made more sense if Tlacey owned its contract, and had sent it here to kill Tapan.

If it tried to attack my client, I would tear it apart.

Tapan, sitting on the pad and watching me worriedly, mouthed the words, "What is it?"

I opened a secure channel to her and said, *Someone is outside the door. I'm not sure why.*

That was mostly true. I didn't want to tell Tapan what it was, since that seemed to lead directly to me telling her what I was, which I didn't want to do. Though if I had to destroy it in front of her, I was going to have a lot of explaining to do.

The sexbot replied, *This is you,* and sent me a copy of a public newsburst.

It was from the station, from Port FreeCommerce. This time the headline was "Authorities Admit a Sec-Unit Unsecured and Location Unknown."

Uh-oh, ART said.

I closed the story by reflex, like that would make it not exist. After three seconds of shock, I made myself open it again.

"Unsecured" is what they call rogue SecUnits when they want humans to listen and not just start screaming. It meant that the knowledge that I had hacked my governor module was no longer confined to me and the members of PreservationAux. They must have been at the stage where everyone in the two survey groups who had survived was being interviewed, and they would have had to guarantee bonds to assert they were telling the truth.

So the company knew now that I had hacked my governor module. That was terrifying, even though I had expected it. It was one of the reasons Mensah had made sure to get me off inventory and out of the deployment center as soon as I came out of repair and reconstruction mode.

Expecting it and having it happen were two different things, something I learned the first time I got shot to pieces.

I skimmed the story in dread and then read it again, closely. The solicitors for several sides in the ongoing legal and civil battles had asked Preservation to produce the SecUnit who had recorded all the damning evidence against GrayCris. This was unusual. It's not like SecUnits can testify in courts. Our recordings are admissible, just like recordings from a drone or security camera or any other inert device, but it's not like we're supposed to have opinions or a perspective on what we record.

After some back and forth, Mensah's solicitor had admitted that she had lost track of me. They phrased it as "released on my own recognizance, as constructs are considered legal sentients under Preservation law," but the journalists hadn't been fooled by that, either. There were a lot of sidebar links to attached articles about constructs, about SecUnits, about rogue SecUnits. There was no mention that this particular unit had had a little problem with murdering the clients supposedly under its protection before, but I had the feeling the company had probably already destroyed any records relating to Ganaka Pit so they couldn't be produced under court injunction.

Tapan whispered, "Are you talking to them, the person?"

"Yes," I told her. To the sexbot, I said, *That's an interesting story but it has nothing to do with me.*

It said, *It's you. Who sent you?*

I said, *That's a story about a dangerous rogue SecUnit. No one would send it anywhere.*

I'm not asking because I want to report you. I won't tell anyone. I'm asking—There's no human controlling you? You're free?

I could feel ART in my feed, carefully extending itself out toward the sexbot.

I have a client, I told it. I had to distract it, if ART was going to be able to get any info. Even though it was a sexbot, it was still a construct, still a whole different proposition from a pilot bot. *Who sent you here? Was it Tlacey?*

Yes. She is my client.

As a ComfortUnit, not a SecUnit. Sending a ComfortUnit into this situation was morally irresponsible and a clear violation of contract. I'm guessing the sexbot knew that.

ART said, *It's not rogue. Its governor module is engaged. So it's probably telling the truth.*

I asked ART, *Can you hack it from here?*

There was a half-second pause while ART explored the idea. ART answered, *No, I can't secure the connection here. It could stop me by cutting off its feed.*

I told the sexbot, *Your client wants to kill my client.*

It didn't reply.

I said, *You told Tlacey about me.* It must have recognized what I was during that first meeting. If it hadn't been sure, seeing the damage I had done to the three humans Tlacey had sent would have been all the confirmation it needed. I was seething, but I kept it out of the feed. As I told ART, bots and constructs can't trust each other, so I don't know why it made me angry. I wish being a construct made me less irrational than the average human but you may have noticed this is not the case. I said, *Your client sent a ComfortUnit to do a SecUnit's job.*

It countered, *She didn't know she needed a SecUnit until today.* It added, *I told her you were a SecUnit, I didn't tell her you were a rogue.*

I wondered if I could believe that. And I wondered if it had tried to explain to Tlacey the impossibility of this assignment. *What do you propose to do?*

There was a pause. A long one, five seconds. *We could kill them.*

Well, that was an unusual approach to its dilemma. *Kill who? Tlacey?*

All of them. The humans here.

I leaned against the wall. If I had been human, I would have rolled my eyes. Though if I had been human, I might have been stupid enough to think it was a good idea.

I also wondered if it knew a lot more about me than what little was in the newsburst.

Picking up on my reaction, ART said, *What does it want?*

To kill all the humans, I answered.

I could feel ART metaphorically clutch its function. If there were no humans, there would be no crew to protect and no reason to do research and fill its databases. It said, *That is irrational.*

I know, I said, *if the humans were dead, who would make the media?* It was so outrageous, it sounded like something a human would say.

Huh.

I said to the sexbot, *Is that how Tlacey thinks constructs talk to each other?*

There was another pause, only two seconds this time. *Yes.* Then, *Tlacey believes you stayed behind to steal the files for the tech group. What did you do for so long in the feed blackout area?*

I was hiding. I know, not my best lie. *Does Tlacey know you want to kill her?* Because the "kill all humans" thing might have come from Tlacey, but the intensity under it was real, and I didn't think it was directed at all humans.

She knows, it said. Then *I didn't tell her about your cli-*

*ent, she thinks they all left on the shuttle. She only wanted
me to follow you.*

A code bundle came through the feed. You can't infect
a construct with malware like that, not without sending
it through a Sec or HubSystem. Even then I would have
to apply it, and without direct orders and a working governor module, there's no way to force me to do it. The
only way that code can be applied without my assistance
is through a combat override module via my dataport.

It might be killware, but I was not a simple pilot bot,
and it would mostly just annoy the hell out of me. Maybe
to the point where I tore a door off the wall and ripped
the head off a ComfortUnit.

I could just delete the bundle, but I wanted to know
what it was so I knew how furious to get. It was small
enough for a human's interface to handle, so I shunted it
aside to Tapan. I said aloud, "I need you to isolate that for
me. Don't open it yet."

She signaled assent through the feed and pulled the
bundle into her temp storage. The other thing about killware and malware is that they can't do anything to
humans or augmented humans.

The sexbot hadn't said anything else and I sent a ping
in time to feel it withdraw its feed. It was walking away
down the corridor.

I waited until I was sure, then stepped back from the

door. I debated staying here, or moving Tapan. Now that I knew something was hacking the security cameras to watch me, I could use countermeasures. I probably should have been doing that from the beginning, but you may have noticed that for a terrifying murderbot I fuck up a lot.

"It's gone," I told Tapan. "Can you check out that code bundle for me?"

She got that inward look that humans have when they're deep in their feed. After a minute, she said, "It's malware. Pretty standard ... Maybe they thought it would get your augments, but that's kind of amateurish for Tlacey. Hold it. There's a message string in here, attached to the code."

ART and I waited. Tapan's face did something complicated, settling on worry. "This is weird." She turned to the display surface and made the completely unnecessary gesture that some humans can't help doing when they send something from their feed to display.

It was the message string, three words. *Please help me.*

I moved us to a different room, near an emergency exit, in another section of the hostel. The sexbot might be alert for hacking, so I removed the access plate, manually broke the lock, and replaced the plate again while Tapan

watched the corridor. Once we were inside, I told Tapan
some of what the sexbot had said, mostly the part about
how it claimed Tlacey didn't know Tapan was here. (I
didn't tell her our visitor had been a sexbot because
Tlacey had figured out what I was and didn't want to
waste any more human bodyguards on me.) "But we don't
know that that's true, or that this operative won't tell
Tlacey you're here now."

Tapan looked confused. "But why did they tell you
anything?"

That was a good question. "I don't know. They don't
like Tlacey, but that might not be the only reason."

Tapan bit her lip, considering. "I think I should still try
to keep the meeting. It's only four hours from now."

I'm used to humans wanting to do things that can get
them killed. Maybe too used to it. I knew we should leave
now. But I needed time to hack enough of the security
system to get past the sexbot. Once I did that, it seemed
wrong not to wait the short time to make the meeting,
which Tapan was reasonably sure Tlacey didn't know
about. Reasonably sure.

It was probably a trap.

I needed to think. I told Tapan I was going to sleep for
a while and laid down on my side on my section of padding. My recharge cycle isn't obvious but it doesn't look
like a human sleeping, so what I was actually going to do

was play some media in the background of my feed while I worked on my security countermeasures and looked up my old module on risk assessment.

Thirty-two minutes later, I heard movement. I thought Tapan was getting up to go to the restroom facility, but then she settled on the pads behind me, not quite touching my back. I had set my breathing to sound deep and even, like a human sleeping, with occasional random variations to add verisimilitude, so the fact that I had frozen in place wasn't obvious.

I had never had a human touch me, or almost touch me, like this before and it was deeply, deeply weird.

Calm down, ART said, not helpfully.

I was too frozen to respond. After three seconds, ART added, *She's frightened. You are a reassuring presence.*

I was still too frozen to answer ART, but I upped my body heat. Over the next two hours, she yawned twice, breathed deeply, and snorted occasionally. At the end of that time I changed my breathing and moved a little, and she immediately slid off my pad and over to hers.

By that time, I had a plan, sort of.

I convinced Tapan that I should go to the meeting, and she should get on a public shuttle to the transit ring immediately. She was reluctant. "I don't want to abandon you," she said. "You're only involved in this because of us."

That hit home so hard my insides clenched. I had to lean over and pretend to look through my bag to hide my expression. Company emergency protocol allows clients to abandon their SecUnits if necessary, even in situations where the company might never be able to retrieve them. Tapan was making me think of Mensah, yelling that she wouldn't leave me. I said, "It'll help me the most if you go back to the transit ring."

It took a while, but I finally convinced her this was for the best for both of us.

Tapan left the hostel first, wearing both extra jackets from her pack to change her body shape and with the hood of one pulled up to conceal her hair and shadow her face. (This was mostly to make her feel more confident, and because I didn't want to explain the extent to which I could gain temporary control over portions of Ravi-Hyral's admittedly not-great security system.) I watched her on the security cameras until I saw her reach the public dock about one hundred meters away, go down the walkway to the embarkation area, then board the shuttle that was scheduled to leave in twenty-one minutes. ART sent me an acknowledgment as it slid into the shuttle's controls to guard the bot pilot again. Then I left the hostel.

I'd prepared a hack for the security cameras that was much more sophisticated than the one I'd been using up to this point. It involved getting into the operational code and setting the system on a tenth of a second delay, then deleting Tapan out and randomly replacing that part of the recording with pieces cut from earlier. This would work because the sexbot would be scanning the recordings the same way I would, using a body configuration scan. I didn't match SecUnit standard anymore, but the sexbot had had plenty of time to scan my new configuration during that first meeting with Tlacey.

Right now I wanted the sexbot's attention on me, and not the public dock. I let the cameras track me out of the port and back toward the tube access. Then I started the hack.

I was only 97 percent certain this meeting was a trap.

Chapter Eight

WHEN I REACHED THE small food service counter in the contractor district, a human was there who matched the image Tapan had sent to my feed. As I sat down at the table he looked up at me, his expression nervous, sweat beading on his pale forehead. I said, "Tapan couldn't come," and sent his feed the brief recording Tapan had made with her interface. It was her standing next to me in the room at the hostel, holding my arm and explaining that the files could be given to me. Wow, I looked uncomfortable.

His gaze went inward as he reviewed the recording, then his body relaxed a little. He slid a memory clip over to me. I took it and checked the cameras.

Nothing. No potential threats, no one showing interest in us. The counter served drinks with a lot of bubbles in them and fried protein in the shape of water fauna and flora. Everyone else was busy eating or talking. There was no one suspicious in the corridor or mall area outside, no one watching, no one waiting.

This was not a trap.

The human said uncertainly, "Should we order something? To make it look like we're not—you know?"

I told him, "No one's watching, you can leave," and pushed to my feet. I had to get back to the port.

If this wasn't a trap, the real trap was somewhere else.

———————

On the way back to the dock, I checked the schedule. The shuttle was now listed as delayed.

As I reached the embarkation area, I was reviewing the security recording from the time Tapan had boarded the shuttle. On visual, I spotted the sexbot coming toward me from the far end of the walkway.

I had gotten to the point in the recording where two humans with Port Authority identification had stopped the shuttle's departure and removed Tapan. ART slid out of the shuttle and back into my feed. It said, *If I had my armed drones, this would be easier.*

When the sexbot reached me, I said, "Where is she?"

"In Tlacey's private shuttle. I'll show you."

I followed it along the walkway, then down the ramp that split off toward the private shuttle docks. ART said, *Why is it showing you where your human is?*

I said, *Because Tlacey doesn't want Tapan, she wants me.*

ART was quiet as we went past the private shuttle

slots toward the bigger, more expensive section at the end. Then it said, *Retrieve your human and make Tlacey regret this.*

We stopped in front of the access to a shuttle hatch. No one was outside, and most of the activity was down toward the other end of the docks. The sexbot turned to face me.

It opened its hand, and I recognized the small object. It was a combat override module. It said, "They won't allow you aboard unless you let me install this."

In my feed, ART said, *Ah.*

They wanted us in the shuttle so that they could dispose of the bodies. Or Tapan's body. Me they obviously intended to keep.

A combat override module contains code that will take over my system, overriding the governor module and the company factory-set protocols, and placing me under the direct verbal or comm control of whoever the module designates. This was how GrayCris took over DeltFall's SecUnits, and tried to take over me.

I said, "If I accept that, will they release my client?"

In the feed the sexbot whispered, *You know they won't.* Aloud, it said, "Yes."

I turned and let it insert the module into my data port. (The data port that ART had disconnected when it altered my configuration. With my governor module hacked, it had been the only way left to assert control over me, so disabling it had been a priority.)

The module clicked into place and I had a moment of purely irrational fear. ART must have picked up on it because it said, *Please, my MedSystem makes no mistakes.* Nothing happened, and from the security camera I had control of, I saw that I managed to keep the relief out of my expression.

The sexbot's expression was Unit standard neutral, and I followed it into the shuttle. A human stood just inside the lock, armed, his eyes flicking nervously between me and the sexbot. He said, "Is it under control?"

"Yes," the sexbot said.

He stepped back and his jaw moved as he spoke in his feed. I couldn't hack anything without the sexbot knowing, so I waited. I kept my expression blank. I had no way of knowing what the combat override module was supposed to make me do, but I was assuming it would put me under Tlacey's control. I suspected the humans, and the sexbot, weren't sure what the outward effect would be.

Once we were through the lock, it cycled shut and a launch warning went through the feed, ending in an audible beep from the comm system. Tlacey must have bribed someone for immediate clearance, because there was a clunk as the lock disengaged and then the shuttle slid out of its slot.

I have you on my scan, ART said.

The human led the way through the shuttle. It was a large model, and the access corridor went past hatchways to cabins and the engineering section before ending in a big compartment. There was cushioned bench seating against the walls and acceleration chairs to the front, near the hatch that must lead to the forward part of the ship. There were six unknown humans in the room, four armed and two unarmed crew. One of the armed humans held Tapan by the shoulder and had a projectile weapon pressed to her head.

Tlacey stood up from a chair and looked me over with a smile. She said, "Take little Tapan to a cabin. I'll want to talk to her later about her work."

Tapan's eyes were wide and frightened. I kept my expression blank. She tried to say, "Eden, I'm sorry! I'm sorry—" but the guard pulled her through another hatchway and down a corridor. I didn't react, since I wanted her out of the line of fire. I listened for the hatch to close, then focused on Tlacey.

She strolled toward me, thoughtful now. I guess the triumphant smile had been for Tapan's benefit. The two other unarmed humans were watching with nervous curiosity, the armed guards still looked cautious. To the sexbot, Tlacey said, "You really think this is one of the units from the Ganaka Pit accident?"

ately, Tlacey relaxed and grinned. "I like a mouthy bot. This is going to be interesting—"

ART was in the shuttle's systems and I was clear. I caught the sexbot's arm and flung it across the room toward the three armed guards. One went down, one stumbled into a chair, the third started to lift his weapon. I knocked Tlacey out of my way and stepped on the sexbot as I went over it, thumping it back down to the deck. I grabbed the muzzle of the energy weapon and shoved it upright just as he fired. The discharge struck the curved ceiling. I ripped it out of his grasp, dislocating his shoulder and at least three fingers, and slammed his head down on the console.

The guard who had already fallen to the deck had a projectile weapon and I felt two impacts, one to my side and one to my thigh. Now that's the kind of attack that actually hurts. I extended my right arm and fired my inbuilt energy weapon, catching him with two bolts in the chest. I stepped sideways to avoid an energy weapon blast from the guard who had fallen into the chair, and my third shot hit him in the shoulder. I had the blasts set to narrow, and they created deep burn wounds that usually incapacitated humans rapidly with shock and pain and, you know, having holes burned into their chest cavities.

I pivoted and threw the captured gun as a distraction.

The first unarmed human was on the deck, a smoking wound in her back; the guard who had missed me had shot her. The second flung herself across the compartment to try to grab a fallen projectile weapon, so I shot her in the shoulder and the leg.

The sexbot rolled to its feet and charged me, I caught it, went down on my back, and flung it off and over my head. I twisted around and up to my knees but couldn't get all the way up due to the wound in my right thigh. The sexbot shoved upright and I grabbed its leg and popped the knee out of the socket. It went down and I took out its left shoulder joint. Slamming it down to the deck, I turned to see Tlacey reaching for one of the fallen weapons. I said, "Touch that weapon and I'll take it away from you and insert it into your rib cage."

She froze. She was panting from fear, eyes staring. I said, "Tell your sexbot to stop fighting."

It was still struggling to get up and it was just going to hurt itself further. Especially if it made me mad again.

Tlacey straightened slowly, her jaw working, and the sexbot relaxed. I said, *ART, cut off Tlacey's feed.*

Done, ART said.

Tlacey winced as her feed went down. I told Tlacey, "Give the sexbot a verbal command to obey me until further notice. Try to give it any other command and I'll rip your tongue out."

Tlacey huffed out a breath, then said, "Unit, obey the crazy rogue SecUnit until further notice." To me, she said, "You need to get better threats."

I put a hand on the nearest chair seat and shoved myself to my feet. "I don't make threats, I'm just telling you what I'm going to do."

Her jaw hardened. Two of the humans in the room had stopped breathing, the unarmed one that the guard had shot while aiming for me and the first one I had shot. Tlacey hadn't noticed.

I looked down at the sexbot, which looked up at me. "Stay down," I said.

It sent me an acknowledgment. I stepped over it, grabbed Tlacey's arm, and dragged her down the corridor to the cabin where her guard had taken Tapan.

She said quickly, "So you're a free agent, right? I can give you a job. Whatever you want—"

I thought, *You don't have anything I want.* I said, "All you had to do was give them the fucking files and none of us would be in this situation."

The look she threw back at me was startled, incredulous. I didn't sound like her idea of a SecUnit, rogue or otherwise, I guess.

Humans should really do more research. There were operating manuals that would have warned her not to fuck with us.

Tlacey stopped at a closed hatch, said, "Bassom, it's me," and hit the release. The door slid up.

Tapan was half sprawled across the bunk on the far wall, blood spreading across the flower pattern on her T-shirt, drops of it splashed on the brown skin of the bare arm pressed against the wound in her side. Her raspy breath sounded loud in the small cabin. The bodyguard stared at us, eyes wide.

"He panicked when he heard the shots," Tlacey gasped. "You can't—"

Oh yeah, I could.

I swung Tlacey to shield me as the bodyguard brought up his weapon. Multiple shots hit her back but I'd already crushed her windpipe. I took another projectile in the chest as I crossed the cabin, threw him against the wall, jammed my arm up under his chin, and triggered my energy weapon.

I stepped back and let his body drop.

I turned away from it and leaned over Tapan. I said, stupidly, "It's me." Her eyes were shut and she was breathing through gritted teeth. I clamped my hand over the wound to stop the bleeding and said, *ART, help.*

ART said, *I've been guiding the shuttle toward the transit ring, where I can dock it with myself. ETA is seventeen minutes. MedSystem is prepping for your arrival.*

I sank down beside Tapan. She was just conscious

enough to reach over and squeeze my hand. I pulled the useless combat override module out of the back of my neck and tossed it away.

I had made a huge mistake, which seemed blindingly obvious in hindsight. I had known the invitation to exchange the signing bonus for the files was a trap from the beginning and I should have convinced Rami and the others not to return to RaviHyral. The augmented human security consultant I was pretending to be would have done that. I was used to taking orders from humans and trying to mitigate whatever damage their stupid ideas did to them, but I had wanted to work with a group again, I had enjoyed how they had listened to me, I had put my need to get to RaviHyral above the safety of my clients.

I was just as shit at being a security consultant as any human.

Chapter Nine

BY THE TIME WE were on approach to the transit ring, ART had cleared us with the ring's Port Authority. Shuttles weren't supposed to be able to dock with transports without advance notice, but ART took care of approach permission, and forged its captain's feed signature to pay the fine for not giving prior notice of the scheduled trip. They didn't suspect anything; nobody knew transports could have bots sophisticated enough to fake being human in the feed. I sure hadn't known it.

The locks weren't compatible but ART solved that problem by pulling the shuttle into an empty module meant for lab space. It sat us down, filled the module with atmosphere, and then cycled our lock. I got upright and carried Tapan out and up the access into the main section. ComfortUnit followed me.

The MedSystem was ready by the time I walked in and laid Tapan down on the platform. Drones whizzed around me and I picked up the MedSystem feed's instruction to remove her shoes and clothes. As the cradle closed around her, I sank down beside the platform.

She was out now, the MedSystem keeping her under while it finished its assessment and started to work. Two medical drones flew around me, one diving in toward my shoulder and the other poking at the wound in my thigh. I ignored them.

A larger drone flew in, carrying Tapan's bag, her blood-stained jacket, and my knapsack. ART flashed me a view of the other drones still inside the shuttle. Four of the humans in the shuttle were still alive, though unconscious. ART had sent drones to scrub and sterilize away my fluids and Tapan's blood from the shuttle's interior. ART had already wiped the bot pilot's memory and deleted any security data. It was also chatting casually with transit ring launch authority with a forged feed signature from one of the dead humans.

I watched as the drones finished and retreated, then ART sealed the shuttle again and launched it with a filed flight plan back to RaviHyral. The onboard bot pilot would land it, full of terribly injured humans, and no one would know they hadn't done it to each other until they were all conscious and told their stories. Though maybe some wouldn't want to tell the story of how they had helped kidnap another human. Whatever happened, it would give us all time to get out of here.

I asked ART, *How did you know to do that?* though I already knew the answer.

It knew I knew, but it said, *Episode 179 of* The Rise and Fall of Sanctuary Moon.

ComfortUnit knelt beside me. "Can I help?"

"No." The medical drones were clamped onto me now, digging for the projectiles, and I was leaking onto ART's pristine MedSystem floor. The anesthetic was making me numb. "How did you know I was one of the Ganaka Pit units?"

It said, "I saw you get off the tube access in that section. There's nothing else down there. It's not in the historical database anymore, but the humans still tell each other horror stories about it. If you were really a rogue and not under orders to go there, then there was an eighty-six percent chance that you went there because you were one of the units involved."

I believed it. "Drop your wall."

It did, and I rode the feed into its brain. I could feel ART with me, alert for traps. But I found the governor module, rendered it null, and slid back out into my own body again.

The ComfortUnit had fallen back, sitting down on the deck with a thump, staring at me.

I said, "Go away. Don't let me see you again. Don't hurt anyone on this transit ring or I'll find you."

It shoved upright, unsteady. More of ART's drones flicked through the air, making sure it didn't try to damage anything, herding it toward the door. It followed the drones out into the corridor. Through ART's feed I watched it go through to the main hatch, where the lock cycled and it went out into the transit ring.

ART watched it walk away through its lock camera. It said, *I thought you might destroy it.*

Too tired and numb to talk, I signaled a negative through the feed. It hadn't had a choice. And I hadn't broken its governor module for its sake. I did it for the four ComfortUnits at Ganaka Pit who had no orders and no directive to act and had voluntarily walked into the meat grinder to try to save me and everyone else left alive in the installation.

ART said, *Now get on the other platform. The shuttle will land soon and there is a great deal of evidence to destroy.*

———

When Tapan woke, I was sitting on the MedSystem's platform holding her hand. The MedSystem had taken care of my wounds, and I'd cleaned off all the blood. The projectiles that had hit me and the energy bursts from my own weapons had left holes in my clothes, and ART had produced a new set for me from its recycler. It was basically ART's crew uniform without the logos: pants with lots of sealable pockets, a long-sleeved shirt with a collar just high enough to cover my data port, and a soft hooded jacket, all of it either dark blue or black. I fed my bloody clothes into the recycler so the waste-reclamation levels would be neutral and ART wouldn't have to forge its log.

Tapan blinked up at me, confused. "Um," she said, and squeezed my hand. The drugs made her expression bleary. "What happened?"

I said, "They tried to kill us again. We had to leave. We're back on the transit ring, on my friend's ship."

Her eyes widened as she remembered. She winced, and muttered, "Fuckers."

"Your friend was telling the truth, he gave me your files." I held up the memory clip, and showed her I was putting it into the interface pocket in her bag. I'd checked it already for malware or tracers. "This ship has to leave soon. I need you to call Rami and Maro to come meet us outside the embarkation zone."

"Okay." She fumbled at her ear, and I handed her the blue feed interface. One of ART's drones had found it in Tlacey's pocket. She took it, started to put it back in her ear, and hesitated. "They're going to be so mad."

"Yeah, they are." I thought they would be so glad to have her alive it wouldn't occur to them to be angry.

She winced again. "I'm sorry. I should have listened to you."

"It wasn't your fault."

Her brow crinkled. "I kind of think it was."

"It was my fault."

"It's both our faults then, but we won't tell anybody," Tapan decided, and wiggled the interface into her ear.

———

I did a quick walk-through of the areas of the ship I had used, to make sure nothing was out of place. ART's drones had already come through, taking Tapan's bloody clothes to be cleaned and sterilizing surfaces so any attempt to collect trace evidence would fail. Not that ART intended to be here when the investigation started. We were all leaving immediately, but ART believed in contingency plans. I started to remove the comm interface ART had given me. "You need to clean this, too."

No, ART said. *Keep it. Maybe we'll come within range of each other again.*

The MedSystem had already sterilized itself and deleted the records of my configuration change and the emergency trauma treatments to both me and Tapan. I was waiting for her when she came out of the bath facility. Drones followed her in to clean away any traces of her presence, and she said, "I'm ready." She had stuffed her old clothes into her pack and was wearing fresh ones. She still looked a little bleary.

We walked out together and the lock sealed behind us. I had the cameras in the embarkation zone and ART was already doctoring the security recordings on its lock to erase our presence.

We met Rami, Maro, and the rest of their group at a food stand outside the embarkation zone. Rami had messaged me that they had already bought passage on a passenger transport leaving within the hour. They greeted Tapan enthusiastically, with tears and admonishments to each other not to squeeze her too hard.

I'd told them already not to talk about it in public. Rami turned and handed me a hard currency card. "Your friend Art said this was a good way to pay you."

"Right." I took it and tucked it in a sealable pocket.

They were all watching me now and it was a little nerve-racking. Rami said, "So, you're going?"

I had my eye on a cargo transport heading the right direction. With luck I should be leaving within minutes of their departure. "Yes, I should hurry."

"Can we hug you?" Maro let go of Tapan and faced me.

"Uh." I didn't step back, but it must have been obvious the answer was no.

Maro nodded. "Okay. This is for you." She wrapped her arms around herself and squeezed.

I said, "I've got to go," and walked away down the mall.

Fading, already disengaging from its lock, ART said in my feed, *Be careful. Find your crew.*

I tapped the feed in acknowledgment, because if I tried to say anything else I was going to sound stupid and emotional.

I didn't know what I was going to do now, if I was going to go ahead with my plan or not. I had hoped finding out what had happened at Ganaka Pit would clear everything up, but maybe revelations like that only happened in the media.

Speaking of which, I needed to grab some more downloads before my next transport left. It was going to be a long trip.

Read on for an excerpt from
the next novella in the Murderbot Diaries

ROGUE PROTOCOL
Available Now

I HAVE THE WORST luck with bot-driven transports.

The first one had let me stow away in exchange for my collection of media files, with no ulterior motives, and had been so focused on its function that there had been hardly more communication between us than you'd have with a hauler bot. For the duration of the trip I had been alone with my media storage, just the way I like it. It had spoiled me into thinking all bot transports would be like that.

Then there was Asshole Research Transport. ART's official designation was deep space research vessel. At various points in our relationship, ART had threatened to kill me, watched my favorite shows with me, given me a body configuration change, provided excellent tactical support, talked me into pretending to be an augmented human security consultant, saved my clients' lives, and had cleaned up after me when I had to murder some humans. (They were bad humans.) I really missed ART.

Then there was this transport.

It was also bot-driven, no crew, but it carried passengers,

mostly minimum to moderately skilled tech workers, human and augmented human, traveling to and from transit stations on temporary work contracts. This was not an ideal situation for me, but it was the only transport going in the right direction.

Like bot-transports that were not ART, it communicated in images and had allowed me onboard in exchange for a copy of my stored media. Because the manifest was in the transport's feed and so available to the other passengers, I asked it to list me for the duration of the voyage in case anybody checked. There was a field in the passenger form for occupation and in a moment of weakness, I told it I was a security consultant.

Transport decided that meant it could use me as onboard security and started alerting me to problems among the passengers. I was an idiot and started responding. No, I don't know why, either. Maybe because it was what I was constructed to do and it must be written into the DNA that controls my organic parts. (There needs to be an error code that means "I received your request but decided to ignore you.")

Initially, it had been pretty easy. ("If you bother her again I will break every individual bone in your hand and arm. It will take about an hour.") Then it had gotten more complicated as even the passengers who liked each other started to get into fights. I spent a lot of time (valuable time I could have been viewing/reading my saved enter-tainment media) arbitrating arguments I didn't give a shit about.

Now it was the last cycle of the trip, all of us somehow having managed to survive, and I was heading into the mess compartment to break up yet another fight between idiot humans.

Transport didn't have drones, but it did have a limited range of security cameras, so I knew the positions of everybody in the galley/mess area before the door slid open. I strode across the room, through the maze of shouting humans and overturned tables and chairs, and stepped between the two combatants. One had picked up a food utensil as a weapon and in one careful non-finger-ripping-off twist I had it, instead.

You would think the person they knew as a security consultant slamming in and disarming one of them would cause everyone to stop and reassess their priorities in this situation, but oh, you would be wrong. They staggered back, still screaming profanity at each other. The others in the room switched from shouting profanity at the com-batants to shouting at me, all trying to tell me different versions of what had happened. I yelled, "Shut up!"

(The good thing about pretending to be an augmented human security consultant instead of a construct Sec-Unit is that you can tell the humans to shut up.)

Everybody shut up.

Then, still breathing hard, Ayres said, "Consultant Rin, I thought you said you didn't want to come back up here—"

The other one, Elbik, was pointing dramatically. "Consultant Rin, he said he was going to—"

I'd had Transport list my name as Rin on the manifest though I'd used Eden at RaviHyral. I was fairly certain RaviHyral transit station security had no reason to associate that identity with any sudden deaths taking place on a private shuttle, and even if they had, wouldn't pursue anyone out of their jurisdiction unless contracted to. But it had seemed best to change it.

The others, starting to come out from behind tables and hastily assembled chair barricades, all tried to chime in, and there was more pointing and shouting. This was typical. (If it wasn't for the shows I download from the entertainment feed, I would have thought the only way most humans knew how to communicate was by pointing and shouting.)

The objective twenty-six cycles of the journey had felt like a subjective two hundred and thirty, at least. I had tried to distract them. I had copied all my visual media into Transport's passenger-accessible system so it could be played on all their display surfaces, which at least kept the crying to a minimum (for children and adults). And, granted, the fighting had decreased dramatically after the first time I pinned someone to a wall with one hand and established a clear set of rules. (Rule Number One: do not touch Security Consultant Rin.) But even that usually left me standing there helplessly listening to their problems and their grievances against each other, against various corporations they had been fucked over by (yeah, tell me about it), and against existence in general. Yes, listening to it was excruciating.

Today, I said, "I don't care."

Everybody shut up again.

I continued, "We have, at most, six hours left before this transport will dock. After that, you can do whatever you want to each other."

That didn't work, they still had to tell me about what had caused the latest fight. (I don't remember what it was, I deleted it from memory as soon as I could get out of the room.)

They were all annoying and deeply inadequate humans, but I didn't want to kill them. Okay, maybe a little.

A SecUnit's job is to protect its clients from anything that wants to kill or hurt them, and to gently discourage them from killing, maiming, etc., each other. The reason why they were trying to kill, maim, etc., each other wasn't the SecUnit's problem, it was for the humans' supervisor to deal with. (Or to willfully ignore until the whole project devolved into a giant clusterfuck and your SecUnit prayed for the sweet relief of a massive accidental explosive decompression, not that I'm speaking from experience or anything.)

But here on this transport, there was no supervisor, just me. And I knew where they were going, and they knew where they were going, even if they were pretending all their anger and frustration was caused by Vinigo or Eva taking an extra simulated fruit pac. So I listened to them a lot and pretended to be launching major investigations into incidents like who left a cracker wrapper in the galley restroom sink.

They were heading to a labor installation on some shitshow world. Ayres told me they had all sold their personal labor for a twenty-year hitch, with a big payout at the end. He was aware it was a terrible deal, but it was better than their other options. The labor contract included shelter, but charged a percentage for everything else, like food consumed, energy use, and any medical care, including preventative.

(I know. Ratthi had said using constructs was slavery but at least I hadn't had to pay the company for my repair, maintenance, ammo, and armor. Of course, nobody had asked me if I wanted to be a SecUnit, but that's a whole different metaphor.)

(Note to self: look up definition of metaphor.)

I had asked Ayres if the twenty years was measured by

the planetary calendar or the proprietary calendar of the corporation who maintained the planet, or the Corporation Rim Recommended Standard, or what? He didn't know, and hadn't understood why it mattered.

Yeah, that was why I was trying not to get attached to any of them.

I would never have picked this transport if I had a choice, but it had been the only one going to the transit station that was the connection to my next destination. I was trying to get to a place called Milu, outside the Corporation Rim.

I had made the decision after I left RaviHyral. At first, I had needed to move fast and put as much distance between myself and its transit station as possible. (See above, murdered humans.) I'd grabbed the first friendly cargo transport and after a seven-cycle trip I disembarked on a crowded transit hub, which was good, because crowds were easy to get lost in, and bad, because there were humans and augmented humans everywhere, all around me, looking at me, which was hell. (After meeting Ayres and the others, obviously my definition of hell changed.)

Also, I missed ART, and I even missed Tapan, and Maro and Rami. If you had to take care of humans, it was better to take care of small soft ones who were nice to you and thought you were great because you kept preventing them from being murdered. (They had only liked me because they thought I was an augmented human, but you can't have everything.)

After RaviHyral, I'd decided to stop screwing around and get out of the Corporation Rim, but I still had to plan my route. The schedules and feeds I needed hadn't been accessible on the transport, but now that we'd docked I was inundated with info, so I had to take some time to go through it all. Plus I had been at this hub for twenty-two minutes and I already desperately needed some quiet time. So I ducked into an automated transient service center and used some of the funds on my new hard currency card to pay for a private rest cubicle. It was just big enough to lay down in with my knapsack, but it was enough like a transport box to be vaguely comforting. I had spent a lot of great alone time in transport boxes, being shipped as freight to contracts. I thought a human had to be pretty tired to rest in here without screaming.

Once I was settled, I checked the station feeds for recently arrived newsbursts about DeltFall and GrayCris. I hit a story thread almost immediately. Lawsuits were underway, depositions in progress, and so on. It didn't look like there had been much change since I left RaviHyral, which was frustrating. That pesky SecUnit nobody wanted to talk about was still unaccounted for, so yay for that. It was hard to tell if the journalists thought somebody was hiding me or not. They didn't seem to want to speculate that I'd wandered off on my own. Then I hit an interview with Dr. Mensah, posted six cycles ago.

It was unexpectedly good to see her again. I increased magnification for a better look and decided she seemed tired. I couldn't tell where she was from the video background and a quick scan of the interview content didn't mention it. I hoped she was back on Preservation; if she was still on Port FreeCommerce I hoped they had contracted decent security. But knowing how she felt about SecUnits (the whole "it's slavery" thing) I doubted she had. Even without a MedSystem on my feed, I could tell there were changes in the skin around her eyes that indicated a lack of sleep verging on chronic.

I felt a little guilty, sort of, almost. Something was wrong, and I hoped it wasn't about me. It wasn't her fault I'd escaped, and I hoped they weren't trying to hold her responsible for, you know, releasing a rogue SecUnit with a record of past mass murder onto an unsuspecting population. Granted, that hadn't been her intention. She had meant to ship me home to Preservation, where she would have, I don't know, civilized me, or educated me, or something. I was vague on the details. The only thing I knew for certain was that Preservation didn't need SecUnits, and their idea of a SecUnit being considered a free agent meant I'd have a human "guardian." (In other places they just call that your owner.)

I reviewed the content again. The investigation of Gray-Cris being conducted by the news agencies was turning up other incidents that suggested the attack on DeltFall was more business as usual for them than an aberration. (This is my surprised face.) GrayCris had been collecting complaints for a long time about sketchy contracts and exclusive-use deals on various sites, including a potential terraforming project outside the Corporation Rim that had been abandoned, though nobody knew why. Fucking up a planet, even part of a planet, for no reason was kind of a big deal, and I was surprised they had gotten away with it. Okay, no, I wasn't surprised.

The journalist asked Dr. Mensah about that last one, and she said, "After what I saw of GrayCris, I intend to urge the Preservation Council to join the formal call to investigate the situation at Milu. A failed terraforming attempt is a tragic waste of both resources and the natural surface of a planet, but GrayCris has refused to explain their actions."

The journalist had tagged an infobar to Mensah's statement, with some commentary about a small company from outside the Corporation Rim which had recently filed to take possession of GrayCris' abandoned terraform project. They had just set up an automated tractor array to prevent the derelict terraform facility from breaking up in the atmosphere, and were supposed to start assessments soon.

The commentary got all dramatic then, wondering what the assessment team would find.

I laid there, flicking through feeds and schedules, and decided I thought I knew what the assessment team would find.

The reason I was wandering free and Dr. Mensah was on the news was because GrayCris had been willing to kill a whole bunch of helpless human researchers for exclusive access to alien remnants, the mineral and possibly biological remains of a sentient alien civilization left in the soil of our survey area. I knew a lot more about it now, after listening to Tapan and the others talk about their code for identifying strange synthetics, and because I'd downloaded a book on it and read it between episodes of my shows. There were tons of agreements between political and corporate entities, inside and outside the Corporation Rim, dealing with alien remnants. Basically you weren't supposed to touch them without a lot of special certifications and maybe not even then.

When I had left Port FreeCommerce, the assumption was that GrayCris had wanted unimpeded access to those remnants. Presumably, GrayCris would have set up a mining operation or colony build or some other kind of massive project as cover while they recovered and studied the remnants.

So what if the terraform facility at Milu was just a

successful cover for a mining or recovery operation for alien remnants or strange synthetics or both? GrayCris had finished the recovery and pretended to abandon the terraform that had never actually been in progress. With the facility derelict, it would eventually break up in the atmosphere, taking all the evidence with it.

If Dr. Mensah had proof of that, the investigation against GrayCris would get a lot more interesting. Maybe so interesting that the journalists would forget all about that stray SecUnit. And then Dr. Mensah wouldn't be needed on Port FreeCommerce and she could go back to Preservation where it was safe and I could stop worrying about her.

Getting proof wouldn't be hard, I thought. Humans always think they've covered their tracks and deleted their data, but they're wrong a lot. So ... maybe I should do that. I could go to Milu and take whatever data I collected and send it to Dr. Mensah, either to wherever she was staying at Port FreeCommerce or to her home on Preservation.

I picked up the hub feed again and changed my queries to search for transports to Milu, but there was nothing on the public schedule for this transit station. I widened my search, checking other connected transit stations. All I could find was an old transportation advisory, tagged forty cycles ago, when the news said the terraform facility had been declared abandoned after the local transit station had registered a lengthy period of inactivity. It said the cargo routes to Milu were discontinued, all except for the route originating at HaveRatton Station, which was on the edge of the Corporation Rim. I couldn't get any updated information about transports going to Milu from HaveRatton, except some vague reports that some had still been in operation at some point.

I might not be able to get to Milu without my own ship, and that wasn't going to happen. I have a training module for hoppers and other planetary aircraft, but not shuttles or transports or anything. I'd have to steal a ship and a bot pilot, and that would just be getting too complicated, even for me.

But HaveRatton was a main hub for transports heading outside the Corporation Rim and I could choose hundreds of destinations from there. So even if the Milu plan turned out to be a bust, it wouldn't be a wasted trip.

The next transport leaving directly for HaveRatton was listed as cargo and passenger, and that's how I ended up with Ayres and his bunch of contract-labor-bound idiots.

About the Author

MARTHA WELLS has written many novels, including the *New York Times* and *USA Today* bestselling Murderbot Diaries series, which has won multiple Hugo, Nebula, Locus, and Alex Awards. Other titles include *Witch King*, *City of Bones*, *The Wizard Hunters*, *Wheel of the Infinite*, the Books of the Raksura series (beginning with *The Cloud Roads* and ending with *The Harbors of the Sun*), and the Nebula Award–nominated *The Death of the Necromancer*, as well as YA fantasy novels, short stories, and nonfiction.